IMMORAL

NICOLE DYKES

FOREWORD

Love whoever you want to love. Be free. Love hard always. And when you're lucky enough to find your person, hold on tight and scream it out loud. Life's too short to hate or to worry about being hated for who you love.

PLAYLIST

Your Song

Ellie Goulding

I Will Buy You a New Life

Everclear

Little By Little

Oasis

Love of My Life

Queen

Angels & Demons

jxdn

Champagne Supernova

Oasis

Smile Like You Mean It

The Killers

High Hopes

Panic! At The Disco

RYAN

"WHAT ARE you doing over here by yourself, loser?"

Grady fucking Bell.

I smile at the sound of my best friend's voice coming from behind me while I sit on the dock, staring at the rippling water in the moonlight. I'm holding onto the neck of a whiskey bottle resting between my legs, but I haven't had much to drink tonight. It's graduation night. I should be happy. I *am* happy.

My dreams are about to come true. So are his.

But those dreams are sending us in completely different directions.

I feel his body crowd mine as he takes a seat on the end of the dock with me, his sneakers dangling just above the water like my own. "There's an epic party going on right back there." He extends his lanky arm behind us, that bigass grin with his bright, white teeth visible in the night.

"Aren't you tired of partying yet, Grady?"

He laughs at that, effortless and contagious. Grady is larger than life. He was even when we were in second grade, never caring what anyone thought about him. He can hit a home run effortlessly. Get an A on a test without even studying. Sing any song in existence acapella while bringing the biggest badass out there to tears. Score the winning touchdown in the last few seconds of a game. Play a song on his guitar perfectly after only hearing it once.

Grady Bell is a goddamn legend in this town, and now he's leaving.

"We're just getting started, Bailey."

I roll my eyes at the use of my last name but still smile because it's something he's always done. *Bell and Bailey*. In a small town like ours, that meant we were always paired together. School. Sports. Newspaper achievements.

Always.

"Seems to me, *Bell*, that we *were* just getting started, but then you had to go and sign with a record label."

He gives me a sly grin and steals the whiskey bottle from between my thighs, even though I can smell the booze on him already. "You want me to tell them to fuck off?" I turn to look at him and that intoxicating grin on his face. "Because I fucking will."

I laugh and look out at the lake water again. We both had baseball scholarships to the same college. That was the plan. It's always been my plan, decided for me before I was even born by a father with the same dream for himself.

Unfortunately, my mom got pregnant in an "oops" situation during their senior year of high school, and my dad proposed, then immediately went to trade school to learn to be a welder. I think it was then he decided I would be the baseball player.

And I'm not half bad.

Grady, the talented motherfucker, is good at all he does and, of course, excelled at baseball along with everything else. So, we decided that was our ticket out of this town. The major leagues. We'd play for the big boys, party like crazy, buy our moms houses, and never come back to this small town.

But instead, he had to go and get signed with a record label who wants him to immediately go to LA and lay tracks for an album. I'm happy for him. Music has always been his favorite talent, but I'm a selfish asshole, feeling lost and abandoned.

"No." I turn to look at Grady, his black hair just a little overgrown and blowing in the wind, and even though I can't see his dark green eyes, I know they're sparkling with mischief. "I want you to go and blow their fucking minds."

His grin widens. "You know I will. And you?"

I shrug and swallow hard, still facing him. "Me?"

"You're going to kill it in college sports, and then you're going to the MLB. You're going to the big leagues, and they won't even know what hit them."

How can I do that without Grady?

What's a catcher without his pitcher?

I don't recognize my own voice as I shift my body so I'm facing him directly, pulling my legs up on the dock and tucking them under me awkwardly. "What if I fail?"

He places the whiskey bottle next to him and then turns his body, mimicking my position. His large hands grip my face, not letting me look away. "Ryan, when have you ever failed in your life?"

When hasn't he been there to back me up? It's what I want to ask, but I don't. I just shake my head, taking his hands with me as I do. "I'm scared."

I hate making this admission. Men don't get scared. And if we do, we sure as hell don't admit it. In a small town like this in

Kansas, men are still supposed to be "tough." We don't show weakness. "Me too."

I'm shocked when he readily admits this. Grady isn't afraid of anything. "You'll be fine."

"I'm going to California, Ry. This is all I've ever known." He doesn't release me, but he looks around the lake. No one is around us, but I hear the music coming from the shabby cabin our class rented for the weekend, and I can see the bonfire they've lit close to it.

"You'll be great."

His eyes meet mine, and I feel that familiar feeling stirring low in my belly. One I've been trying to ignore for years. One I've tried to drink away. I've tried my best to get lost in the girls in our class and out on the baseball field. I've thrown myself into everything else, trying like hell to ignore the one thing I know deep down I want.

Him.

"So will you."

"Chances of going pro are slim," I say lamely, my eyes transfixed on his full lips. No wonder he has such a reputation for being a good kisser. With lips like those, how could he not be?

Of course, that's only with girls.

Every fucking girl in our school.

Grady is, no doubt, straight. And I . . . I have no idea what I am.

Lost.

That seems about right.

He cups the back of my neck with one of his hands and pulls me close, resting his forehead against mine in a gesture he's done a lot when I've doubted myself. "Not for you. You're Ryan fucking Bailey. You're going to go far. You were destined for this."

A shiver runs through me from the intensity of his eyes on mine. "You're always so sure."

"About you? Of course, I am."

I want to lean in even closer. I breathe him in and hope like hell it's not noticeable, but I can't resist. He smells like whiskey and the lake from swimming earlier. And him. Just fucking him.

"Grady?" My voice is full of gravel as he pulls back enough to look into my eyes. His breathing seems rapid, but maybe it's my imagination.

"Yeah?"

I swear his gaze drops to my lips, but I try to shake that thought away. I've wanted him for years, but there's no way he feels the same. "I don't know what I was going to say," I admit.

"You think too much, Bailey. You always have." His thumb on his free hand—the other is still cupping the back of my neck —runs over my bottom lip, and I think I stopped breathing.

When he leans closer to me, I'm almost certain I'm dreaming. Or maybe I fell into the lake and am drowning. *Hell, maybe I'm dead.*

But when his firm lips press against mine, I couldn't give a fuck if I'm actually dead because this is my heaven.

His hand around the back of my neck grips me tighter and pulls me closer as a growl escapes my throat, and I don't think . . . I just attack his mouth with mine. Taking everything I've wanted for so damn long.

My hands move to his thick, soft hair, threading my fingers through it and pulling him to me, not able to get close enough. His mouth opens for me as my tongue darts inside, tasting Grady. *Finally.*

God, he tastes good.

Our moans mingle as he shoves me onto my back on the dock, and I think this is it. This is when he'll wake up from his drunken daze and punch me right in the face.

But he doesn't.

Instead, his body covers mine, settling between my legs, and I know he can feel how hard I am. But what really fucking shocks me to my core, something I'll never forget for as long as I live, is the erection that's *not* mine. His hard dick is pressed against mine as our lips meet again, and we grind against each other. Groaning and moaning with need as we kiss and writhe on the old wooden dock. My body is larger than his—both in pure muscle mass and in height—but he has no problem taking control, grabbing both my hands and pinning them above my head as our clothed cocks rub against each other, and I'm about to lose my mind.

"Grady," I gasp, close to coming in my jeans.

He pulls back enough to look down into my eyes, not releasing his hold on me. "Yeah?"

"What are we doing?"

I could kick myself for stopping this, but this is Grady. He doesn't make out with guys. *I can't be a drunken mistake. Not to him.*

"Celebrating?" His right eyebrow kicks up along with a cocky grin spreading on his too handsome face.

I'm shocked he isn't flipping the fuck out. But again, this is Grady. He doesn't freak out. He's calm, cool, and collected. Always. It's why he's a fucking fantastic pitcher. Nothing rattles him. "Like this?" I rasp as I feel his body on top of mine while I pant and plead with him silently to come back to me.

The spell broken, he sits up, letting go of my wrists and kneeling between my legs. "Maybe not the best idea."

It's like a knife plunging into my heart, but deep down I know he's right. There are so many things I want to say to him. I want to pull him back to me, kiss the fuck out of him, and tell him I'm an idiot for saying anything. To get lost with me.

But I don't. Instead, I take his hand when he stands and then pulls me up, ruffling my hair in the casual, easy way that's just Grady.

He isn't freaking out that he kissed a guy. His thoughts aren't swirling around in his head that's moving far away while I'm staying in the same state where we grew up. He doesn't worry about any of that.

"Come on, fucker. This is our last night before the real world comes calling and we make it our bitch."

I follow, but it's on shaky, uncertain legs.

Because now, I've had a fucking taste. And I have no idea how I'm going to come back from that.

RYAN

7 Years Later

FUCK, what did I do last night?

I reluctantly open my eyes and groan when I see a hand on my chest. A neatly trimmed and manicured nails on a dainty but masculine hand. "Well, hey." The blond guy smiles up at me with a sparkling smile I'm pretty sure attracted to me to him last night.

"Hey." I stretch my arms upward, and the guy takes the opportunity to scoot higher, lying nearly flat against my bare chest.

He traces the tattoo on my bicep. "Lordy, these muscles." He drags his tongue over said muscles, and I try my best not to pull away.

"Yeah?"

"I could stay here and lick them all . . ." he moves down to my pecs, "day . . ." and then the ridges of my sculped abs, "long."

Christ, that thought should make me happy. Or horny. But

really, all I want is to get this guy out of my bed. "As fun as that sounds, I have some things to take care of today."

He pouts, pushing his pink bottom lip out as he looks at me with sad, puppy dog eyes. I could break the guy in two. He's thin and wiry but, if I recall, has a mouth like a fucking hoover. And there's no denying he's a good-looking man. "I suppose you might. But maybe I'll be your good-luck charm."

He winks as I sit up in my bed, pushing him back gently enough to give myself some space. The sheet covers my lap, but that doesn't stop his gaze from going there. "We might need it."

He shakes his head, leaning in to kiss me, but I turn my head because I'm a fucking asshole. He pouts again but quickly recovers. "Game seven is going to be epic. Did you hear who they nabbed for the national anthem?"

That grabs my attention as I climb out of the bed, tugging on a pair of gray sweatpants and turning back to the stranger. "No. Who?"

I don't pay much attention to the entertainment. My mind is on the game. My first World Series. And fuck, if the series hasn't gone all the way to the final game to see who's going to take home the win.

"Immoral. Well, I guess just the lead singer, but it's still pretty damn cool if you ask me." He stands up with no shame at his nakedness, not that he should have any. He tugs on his tight pants from last night and finds his shirt.

"Immoral?"

I sit down on the bed, my legs suddenly too weak to hold me up. "Yeah. Well, Grady Bell."

Fuck.

Me.

Of course, he'll be there. Because why the fuck not? It's only the most important game of my professional career, and I haven't seen him since graduation night seven years ago. But sure, perfect time for a reunion.

"Are you sure? I thought they were on tour."

He grabs his phone, typing away before he shows me an article stating that Grady is back in his "hometown" to finish out the World Series. *Fuck.* Kansas City isn't even our hometown.

We're from a really small town about eighty miles south of Kansas City on the Kansas side, but facts aren't really all that important, right? Not when you're trying to sell something.

"I think their tour ended a couple of weeks ago. Anyway, pretty cool. You're from here too. Do you guys know each other?"

Okay, I'm done with the small talk. "I'm sorry. I really have shit to do. This was fun though."

The guy—for the life of me, I can't remember his name—approaches me, pulling on the waist of my joggers, tugging me closer to him. "Don't be a stranger. I mean, I know I can't say anything about this, but I may have left my name and number in your phone if you're up for more fun."

He kisses me and then tosses me a wink before bouncing out of my room.

Thank God for NDAs. My agent would fucking kill me for last night, but I did get him to sign the NDA before bringing him home and avoided all pictures at the crowded club. And because the World Series happened to be in the town where my house is located, I didn't have to stay in a hotel, so the guy does have my actual address.

Risky. Maybe. But I'm not worried.

Sue me. I was celebrating my team making it to the final game.

But you see, I'm an athlete. And as liberal and accommodating as the sports world tries to seem these days, there are some things that just aren't done as my agent, Jenny, has explained to me many, many times.

My phone rings next to my bed, and I groan, walking over to answer it without even looking. I know who it is this early in the morning. "Hey, Ma."

"Well, hello, Mr. Bigshot World Series Guy."

I roll my eyes but can't help the smile on my face as I take a seat on my bed. My parents are pretty okay even if they may be a little ignorant. But they love me. They always have. They stuck together through the teen pregnancy and managed to have three boys, all baseball players. But I'm the only one that's gone pro so far. Although my youngest brother is well on his way.

"Good morning."

"Did you get enough rest last night?"

I glance at my crumpled sheets and shrug even if she can't see me. "Sure."

"Uh-huh. Well, your father and I are so excited. You know we'll be there in the stands screaming louder than anyone else."

"It's like ninety degrees. Why won't you use your VIP seats? There's air conditioning."

I can actually hear her waving me off. "Please. That's not a real experience. Oh, and did you hear Grady will be there? What ever happened to you two boys? You were so close."

Well, Mom. He kissed my fucking brains out. And then I couldn't handle being in love with a straight guy, so I ditched town early without saying goodbye, and now I'm sure he hates me.

Cannot say that though. "He's busy, Mom."

"Well, you two can catch up. I saw he's dating that cute little girl from that show . . . What's it called?"

"I have no idea, Ma." I do, but I'm not saying it. Grady has had lots of girlfriends over the past seven years. All really high profile celebs like himself.

"Well, maybe you can double-date. If you'd ever bring anyone home, that is. I heard that girl reporter . . . the blonde one that's so cute. What's her name?"

"Veronica." My mom has been trying to set me up with her since she interviewed me my rookie year.

I could go into the whole "Mom, I'm gay" thing again, but what the hell's the point? My mom and dad prefer to live in deliberate ignorance. In their world, their son isn't gay. He's just a player who hasn't quite found the right girl yet.

"Right. Well, I know she's sweet on you."

"I gotta go, Mom. I'll see you later."

"Yes. Go win the World Series, Ry. I'm so proud of you."

"Thanks." I lean back against my headboard, swallowing tightly. She's proud of the baseball player.

But not the man I really am.

GRADY

"You sure you don't want to go another round?" I look over at the gorgeous stranger in my bed, running her painted red fingernail over the tattoos on my ribcage.

"Sorry, sweetie. I have shit to do."

"Right. Super Bowl or some shit." She sits up showing off an amazing pair of tits and making me regret not going for round two. But I actually do have to get going.

I laugh at that. She's funny. "World Series."

"Baseball?" Okay, maybe she's not funny . . .

"Yes." I nod, and she shrugs, finding a shirt from the floor—my shirt—and putting it on. *Damn, that was one of my favorites.*

I already know I'm not getting it back though. "Well, I'll cheer for you. I'm not really a sports person."

Clearly.

"Well thanks, sweetheart. You want me to call you an Uber?"

She finds her skirt from last night, tugging it up and then swinging her bag over her shoulder. "Nah, I can handle it." She leans over the bed, her lips brushing mine. "Call me."

I don't have her number. I don't need it.

"Sure thing."

She winks and walks out of the hotel just as my manager walks in, carrying coffee in both of his hands and wearing a stern expression. The girl giggles as she exits, and Waylon walks toward the king-sized bed in my hotel room. "Really?"

I roll my eyes and hold my hand out for my coffee. "What? I'm not allowed to have fun?"

"You're dating Victoria Bishop, remember?"

He hands me my coffee. I bring it to my lips and take a much-needed drink, sighing when I do. "Yeah, except that I'm fucking not, and you know that."

"Why must you make my life harder than it needs to be?" He flops his 120-pound body onto my bed in his totally dramatic, Waylon way.

"You love the challenge."

He rolls to his side, careful with his own coffee. "That girl has party girl written all over her. She probably took a dick pic."

I shrug. "It's a good dick. I'm not worried."

He scoffs, smiling because Waylon always puts up with my shit. We get along well. He's a good ole southern boy named after an actual country singing legend. But he's barely over a hundred pounds with bright blue eyes and stylish blonde hair, and he loves dick. So, his Bible-thumping parents aren't exactly fans.

Something I can relate to and which made us fast friends as well as client and agent.

"Do I have to spank you?" he teases.

I wiggle my eyebrows. "Careful, you might turn me."

He laughs at that as if it's beyond ridiculous. "You really think that one is going to keep her mouth shut about whatever it is you two did in here last night?"

He looks at the sheets with comical disgust. "What the fuck

do I care? Three orgasms and a big dick is all she can relay. I don't think it will hurt my reputation much."

"Except you're dating Victoria."

"Yeah, I don't think that's going to last much longer."

He groans, "What did you do?"

"Didn't check your social media today, huh? Seems my ex was seen and photographed kissing a girl." I lean in closer as if it's a scandal. "And I think she liked it."

He actually laughs at that. Victoria is a lesbian. She has no interest in dick whatsoever. But the family-friendly show she's been on for five years wasn't having that. So, our agents got together and formed a plan.

One we've both grown sick of over the past couple of months. The show is ending next week. Vicky wants to live her truth, and I'm all for it.

"So, that's it? You're back to bad boy?"

"Wasn't I always?"

Waylon nods, sitting up and taking a drink of his own coffee. "You're going to be the death of me."

"Seriously, what the hell could that chick say that's going to make your life any harder?"

I don't give away anything. I fuck and run. That's it. He knows it. He takes another sip of his coffee and shrugs his small shoulders. "Maybe that you can sometimes be a little . . ." I wait. "Cold?"

"Ouch." I put a hand over my heart, acting wounded. "Fuck you too."

He laughs and then pouts playfully. "Oh, don't be like that. You know what I mean. You have to admit you're a little . . . disconnected. You get what you want, and that's all you worry about."

"I'm not like that with everyone." I know he's mostly joking, but there's a hint of truth there too. I try to shrug it off. "Well, maybe I am, but hey, I care about you. Where's that boyfriend of yours?"

He raises an eyebrow coyly. "Boyfriend?"

"Yeah. Kevin . . . Ken . . . It started with a K."

"Steven?"

I shrug and stand up, not worrying that I'm still naked. He's seen it all before. Probably more than he wants to. He's been responsible for cleaning my drunk ass up way too many times. "Yeah. I was close."

"We broke up months ago."

Well, fuck.

"Sorry," I offer. Maybe I am a little disconnected.

He laughs and climbs off the bed. "No worries. You don't mean to be an asshole. You just are."

"Gee, thanks."

"You ready for tonight?"

To see my ex-best friend? The guy who disappeared and ignored all my attempts to figure out what his fucking problem was?

No.

I'll never be ready for that.

"Singing is what I do. It's no problem."

He eyes me suspiciously even though he doesn't know about Ryan. No one does. I was pretty adamant that I didn't want to do this tonight. But in the end, my record label has me by the balls.

I do what they say when they say it, still paying the price for fame. I sold my soul seven years ago.

"I'll be ready."

"Alright. I suppose I have a shit storm to go clean up."

I chuckle, heading into the bathroom. "Thanks for the coffee, Waylon."

He waves me off as he leaves, and I'm left alone to my thoughts. It's a dangerous place for me—my own head.

Will I even get a chance to see Ry tonight?

Do I even want to?

"WE'RE GOING to do this, boys. It's happening." Bennett wraps his arm around my shoulder as he delivers the pep talk to our team. We're in the locker room, dressed in uniform and about to walk out to our fate.

Bennett is our star pitcher. The pitcher to my catcher on the field only. He's the closest thing I have to a best friend these days and 100 percent straight. Never once has there been a flicker of attraction there, and I'm fucking grateful.

My heart learned long ago not to go down that road.

Still . . . no one—not even Bennett—knows which team I play for off the baseball field.

"Hell yeah, it is!" Kris Mastro, our team's third baseman pumps his fist, already claiming victory. But I'm not so sure.

My stomach is twisted in knots. With Bennett pitching tonight, the odds are in our favor. But anything can happen, and I won't call it a win until it's over.

Bennett's face is overtaken by a massive smile as he points at Mastro. "Hell, yeah! That's the spirit." He drops his arm and pats my ass, shoving me forward. "Where the hell is your head at?"

"It's on the fucking game."

He chuckles, and Mastro nudges my shoulder, aiming a cocky look over at Bennett. "He's probably thinking about all the pussy we're going to get after we win this shit." Couldn't be further from the truth. But of course, I don't say anything. How they haven't figured me out yet, I have no idea. I guess I'm a better actor than I thought when I go out with the guys. But even if I dance and flirt with the women on the dance floor, I've never once left with one. He nudges Bennett. "Unlike you."

Here we go. Bennett, who's happily married and expecting his first kid just grins. "Don't you all ever get tired of the partying bullshit?"

Mastro looks at him as if he's insane and then tucks a beefy arm around my shoulder, tugging me close to him in a frat-bro-style hug, "Hell, no." He turns his head to look at me. "What about you, Bailey?"

"Hell, no. You know me. I'm always up for a party."

I hear the sarcasm in my voice, but I don't think anyone else does. The truth is, I'd much rather go home than to a club these days. I'm tired of the act. Of going to the crowded clubs and watching my teammates search the crowd for the easiest prey while acting like I'm there for the same thing. When really, it's the shy barista at my local coffee shop with green eyes and an ever-present five o'clock shadow or the male sports reporter on the six o'clock news that have captured my attention.

Bennett eyes me a little too long, and I think he might sense my hesitance but doesn't call me on it. "Whatever, losers. While you all are out trolling for pussy, I'll be home with my perfect, gorgeous wife."

"Your wife is hot." Mastro grins, waggling his eyebrows. "Hopefully, she'll soon grow tired of your ass and come to me."

"You're going to get punched before the game. Your agent is going to be pissed if you have to explain that shit," I say with a smirk, and Mastro flips me off before heeding my warning and walking out with the rest of the team.

Bennett is at my side as we trail behind. "We're going to win."

"Let's go warm up." I can't shake my nerves. This is everything I've always wanted. My dad is watching. This is his dream.

I can't blow it.

After warmups, we line up on the field as the crowd goes absolutely insane. Then a man walks out to the middle of the field, waving with an overwhelming, larger-than-life presence.

One he's always had.

Grady fucking Bell.

He's dressed in black ripped jeans with a white tank top showing off his lithe, toned body that's beautifully decorated with swirled ink covering his entire left arm and most of the right. His dark hair is styled in a just-fucked way and his plump lips are made for sin and visible even from the sidelines as he approaches the mic set up on the field only for him.

He owns the crowd, everyone standing and shutting up as he demands attention.

Immoral is a rock band with him as a headliner. They're the real deal. Think the White Stripes, The Killers, and Queen all rolled into one. Grady has no problem singing the national anthem in a way that is 100 percent his own.

The goosebumps that form on my flesh aren't surprising.

That's always happened to me anytime he's opened his mouth to sing any note. When he's done, the crowd goes wild, and we head out for the game of our lives.

But my mind . . .
Yeah . . . it's on the man who's always owned me.

24

GRADY

They won the motherfucking World Series.

My best friend in the world just won the biggest honor in baseball, and I'm not even there to celebrate it with him.

I mean, I was there. I watched as he played a flawless game with not a single error, but it wouldn't surprise me if he didn't even know I was there.

Ryan has always been in his own head. It's why he's so good at baseball. He can focus on the game and tune everything else out, but off the field, he's always overthought every single thing.

It's killing me that he didn't even bother to say hello or even acknowledge my presence. And maybe it's selfish of me, but that pisses me off.

How many nights did we dream of being in the World Series. Of the crowd and the fireworks?

Fuck this.

I call Waylon and beg him to call in a really big favor by securing Ryan's home address, and before I can overthink it—not really a problem for me—-I'm at his gate, ringing the buzzer.

The odds of him actually being home two hours after winning the biggest game of his career are slim, but I'll wait for as long as I have to. While I wait, I look up at the bigass Kansas City mansion secured by an iron gate and smile to myself.

"Damn, Bailey," I whisper.

He's definitely made it. "Hello?"

Well, holy shit. He's home. What if he's not alone?

I shake that off. Why the hell do I care? "Bailey, let me in."

His voice is off, kind of shaky when I hear, "Grady? What the fuck are you doing at my house?"

"Just buzz me in. We need to talk."

There's a pause, and I know he can see me on the security feed he no doubt has. But for me, it's just a voice coming out of a speaker. "No. We don't."

"Yes. We do." I wait a beat. "Are you seriously not going to let me in?"

"Yes."

"Jesus, that's rude. I should call your mother." *Nothing.* I roll my eyes. "Fine, buzz me in or I will sit out here for as long as it takes and give TMZ a call."

I can see his jaw ticking with anger even though I can't actually see him. I feel it. I know him better than I've ever known anyone. Which is why it really fucking sucks that he disappeared, and I still can't pinpoint the reason why.

"Fine."

With that, the lock clicks and the gate opens, allowing me to drive my rental car through the gate. When I park in front, I'm greeted by a pissed-off Ryan, who's flying out his front door in a pair of dark gray joggers and sporting messy bedhead. "Were you seriously asleep at ten o'clock the night after you won the World Series?"

He ignores my question, folding his muscular arms over his chest in a pissed-off stance. "What are you doing here?"

"I want to talk. You gonna let me in?" I look around, knowing there isn't a neighbor close by but also knowing how private Ryan has always been. So, I raise my hands out to my side and say in a loud voice, "Or would you prefer to talk about how you left me without any explanation, all because of one fucking kiss outside on your lawn?"

"Jesus," he hisses, running his fingers through his hair and growling low, "get inside."

He moves out of the way and allows me to shove past him into the wide expanse of a grand foyer. I let out a low whistle. "Sure have come far, haven't you, Bailey?"

I turn to see him glowering at me as he closes the front door. "You're one to talk." Again, he folds his arms over his stomach I can't help but notice is fucking chiseled. He was always pretty built once we started working out in junior high, but now the fucker is solid. No doubt, he spends most of his life in a gym.

I grin. "Yeah, all our dreams came true, huh?"

"Why are you here, Grady?"

"Why did you leave?" It's abrupt and probably not what he was expecting me to ask, but I don't care anymore. I'm tired of wondering.

He scoffs and walks away from me down the foyer, but I grab his bicep. He pulls away, acting like my touch scalded him.

"Jesus Christ, Bailey. I get it, okay? We were drunk off our asses and partying, and it led to a fucking dumbass kiss. You didn't have to fucking bail on me."

He stares at me, his blue eyes threatening to burn through me. "What?"

"What?" I grip the back of my neck, feeling oddly vulnerable. I've never talked about that kiss, but it has to be the reason he left. "It wasn't a big deal. And you kissed me back, FYI, fucker. It's not like it was all me."

He blinks twice and then shakes his head in confusion. "You think I left because a guy kissed me?"

I let out a huff. "And you kissed a guy." I walk closer to him, hating the cold distance he's putting between us. The distance he put there seven years ago. "It's okay. It's not a big deal, but you didn't have to fucking bail."

"I didn't leave because of that."

I stare at him, uncertain and searching my mind for anything else it could have been. "Then why?"

"I thought you were going to freak the fuck out."

I stare at him, me being the confused one now. "Why would I freak out? It wasn't that big of a deal. It was a kiss, man. You didn't have to throw away a longtime friendship over it. I definitely wouldn't have."

"And how did I know that, huh? You aren't gay."

"So." I shrug. "Neither are you."

His eyes flicker with something I almost miss, and then he straightens his back. The fucker is massive. He's broad and made to withstand a grown-ass man barreling toward home plate. "I am."

"You are what?" I cock my head to the side, trying to figure out what the hell is going on. None of the pieces are fitting together.

"I'm gay."

He's what?

RYAN

THIS IS JUST FUCKING GREAT. Exactly what I wanted to deal with tonight.

An angry, confused Grady Bell in my house, demanding answers.

"You can go now," I say to him, hoping for this moment to be over. I can't take him being disgusted or disappointed or whatever the fuck.

I just can't.

I couldn't seven years ago, and I can't today.

"Hold on a second." He holds up his hand, and his face doesn't really say grossed-out, more stunned. "You're gay?"

"Yes." I'm not going to lie. Not to him. Not to the people who are actually in my life. At least not if they ask me outright.

"But . . ." He looks like he's going to be sick now.

That's just great. "I'm not ashamed of it. You can let yourself out."

I try to walk away again, but the asshole reaches out and grips my arm.

Again.

My eyes slice to where he's gripping my bare flesh but then roam to his face. He looks pale. "I've seen you with girls."

I roll my eyes and push his hand away. "Who?"

"Maggie. I saw you two at that party our junior year."

I cringe, thinking about that night. How drunk I was and trying to suppress the feelings that were still raging from seeing Grady in the locker room shower earlier that day. "She was a good kisser but a little soft for me."

"So wait . . ." He's processing, and I'm growing tired of it. But I also let him ask, "If you're gay, why the hell did you freak out about kissing a guy?"

I scoff at that, the sound leaving my lips before I could reel it in. "Not a guy. *You.* My best friend."

"That's fucking worse, asshole. You could have told me." Now he's angry. *Seriously?* "You know I'm not some homophobic asshole. I would have been fine with it."

"Fine?" I laugh coldly, "Gee thanks, Grady."

"You know what I mean. I wouldn't have been a dick. But you just left."

Okay, now he looks hurt. Fuck, I hate that pout. "I was kind of dealing with some shit. You were the first guy I'd kissed. Up until then, I wasn't even totally sure."

His right eyebrow lifts with no caution as a sly grin slowly forms on his lips. "So, I turned you?"

"Holy Christ, you're an idiot." But damn if it doesn't make me laugh. "No. I just wasn't totally sure. When I kissed you, it felt right. Better than with any girl I'd ever tried to kiss."

"Holy shit." He runs a hand over his chin, and I notice his hand has tattoos on it. Tattoos I want to spend time exploring which only proves to me how fast I need to get him out of here.

"Right. So, you can go. Mystery solved."

I start to walk off, but instead of grabbing my arm, the fucker actually grabs both my wrists and slams my body against the wall, pinning me there. "Stop walking away from me."

Holy. Shit. I haven't been this close to him in so goddamn long, but my body remembers, wanting to react. I'm grateful for the space his long, lanky arms allow between our bodies. "Let me go."

"Not until you tell me why the fuck you didn't tell me you were gay."

I'm bigger than him. I still have a few inches on him and at least thirty pounds, but I don't push him away. Always the glutton for punishment. "I couldn't take that sick, disgusted look on your face. It's going to be burned into my brain, so thanks for that."

His brows pinch together in confusion as he continues to plaster my wrists to the wall. "Disgusted? I'm not fucking disgusted. I'm pissed off that you wasted seven years due to a stupid fucking reason. I'm pissed you didn't just tell me you were gay or thought you might be. I don't care who you fuck. I care about you, asshole."

I swallow hard, begging my body not to react to his close proximity, but I can't stop the sharp, jolting pants that are heaving from my chest. Shame heats my cheeks because I know this isn't the full story I'm telling him. It's all so damn humiliating, and he's so relaxed about the whole thing.

I know that Grady isn't an asshole, not like that. I knew then he wouldn't care that I was gay. But the rest of it? *Pining after his straight ass? Yeah. No.*

But I can't tell him that. "I was dealing with a lot of shit, okay? Plus, we were both leaving. I just did it early."

"We weren't planning on not seeing each other. Jesus, man. You wouldn't answer my calls or anything."

I hate the hurt I can see in his eyes now as he drops his hold on my wrists and steps away. "I'm sorry. I know it was shitty."

"It was." His eyes lock on mine. "I'm not my father."

I wince, knowing what a sore subject his prick of a father is. "I know." His father has spent years preaching about love and yet condoning hatred toward anything that he sees as a sin, especially homosexuality.

Then Grady surprises me yet again. "I'm assuming you have a break now that you're a champion?"

"Huh?" I try to get control of my breathing, hating that my physical attraction to him hasn't missed a beat. If anything, it's grown. "Yeah. I have a parade and a couple of appearances, but they're all local. Why?"

He shrugs his shoulders with a cocky grin that's so damn familiar to me. "I have three weeks off too. I think you should invite me to stay."

"What?" I nearly choke out through my shock. "Stay where?"

He makes a show of looking around the grand foyer and then spreads his arms out wide. "Here. It's not like you don't have plenty of room."

"You're insane. We may as well be strangers."

He grabs the back of my neck and pulls me to him, his forehead resting against mine in a gesture that makes me ache from missing it and him so damn much. "We'll never be strangers. I don't care if you push me away for fifty years. I'll always be Bell, and you'll always be Bailey."

"This is a bad idea," I barely whisper.

"I missed you. I want to catch up, and you have a bigass mansion."

"My agent will hate it."

He scoffs at that, stepping back and releasing me. "Are you kidding? Childhood best friends reuniting at the World Series? That's an agent and publicist's wet dream. The media will eat that shit up."

"I try to avoid the media."

"So I've noticed." He smiles, flashing the grin that has probably dropped many, many panties over the years. "Come on, Ry."

Fuck.

"Fine."

"I'm going to go get my bags."

I follow after him as he strides toward the front door. "Wait. You planned this? To come and stay with me after seven years of nothing?"

"No." He grins over his shoulder. "But I had to get out of that hotel they had me in last night and hadn't decided where to stay tonight yet."

I roll my eyes because that's just so fucking Grady.

But I know I'm right, and this is a bad, bad idea.

GRADY

I'M NOT sure what came over me, inviting myself to stay with Ry for a few weeks. But it's always been a gaping hole left in my life. When he left, I was broken. Far more than I ever allowed myself to admit to anyone, even myself.

Now that he's right here, in front of me. I couldn't resist.

He's gay. I couldn't give a fuck. He's still Ryan Bailey.

But I recognize the sad longing in his eyes. It's one I can't and won't ignore. One I see when I've looked at my own reflection for the last seven years.

I grab my bag from the car and walk confidently inside his house where he's still waiting with that same serious scowl on his face. "You're really going to stay here?"

"Give me one good reason why I shouldn't?"

I can see him searching his brain for a reason but just push past him, making sure to nudge his bigass shoulder as I walk by.

"So, where's my room?"

I hear a quick laugh from behind me, and he walks in front of me. "You're still a goddamn asshole."

"Always. Where?"

He nods his head toward the stairs. "There are three guest rooms up there. Take your pick."

"Thanks." I start toward the stairs. "I'll be right back. Then we'll catch up."

I hear him grumbling something about how he was about to go to bed, but I ignore it. He's twenty-five. He can stay up past ten. I go upstairs and find a pristine guest room I'm nearly positive no one has ever stayed in, placing my bag down before leaving the room to go find Bailey.

When I reach the bottom stair, I follow the sounds of glass being moved around which guides me to a large kitchen decorated in stainless steel and where Ry is standing at the fridge. He hands me a beer, unscrewing the lid on his own. "If we're going to catch up, I'm going to need alcohol."

I chuckle at that, twisting the top off mine and taking a much-needed drink. "Damn, that's good."

He's looking at me strangely when I lower the bottle and lock eyes on his. "I can't believe you're here."

I grin and nod toward the glass patio door. "You have a pool."

He looks behind him and nods. "What's a mansion without a pool?"

I grin, thinking about all the times we talked about the things we'd buy when we were famous. Ry always wanted a hot tub. I wanted an underground pool. "What about a hot tub?"

He grins wryly. "Of course. Have to soak my muscles as often as I can."

I'm not sure if he did that on purpose or not, but when he mentions his muscles, I can't stop my eyes from roaming down over his sculpted chest and stomach. Motherfucker is carved out of stone. I'm not sure that's really a requirement in baseball.

His sweats hang low on his hips, and my gaze lingers a little too long on the prominent V of his obliques.

"You okay?"

Fuck. I was not just checking out Ryan Bailey's body.

"I'm fine. How about we go out there to talk? It's a nice night."

"I was in bed."

I grin and start toward the door. "Now you're not."

He grumbles but follows me out onto the patio. We take our seats by the pool. We both sip our beer in quiet contemplation, and I decide to just dive in. Because why not? We've lost seven years.

"So, how the hell did I not know you were gay?"

His look turns into a glare as he turns his head toward me. "What does that mean?"

I roll my eyes when I see he's offended. "Don't get your boxers in a twist. I just mean I can't walk out my door without a fucking camera in my face. They know my every mood. How is it that you fuck dudes and the world doesn't know?"

His shoulders noticeably relax now as he takes a drink of his beer. "I'm not a rockstar, man. They usually report about my stats, not my dating life."

"Yeah, that's total bullshit. I've seen that ugly mug of yours posted all over the fucking place. Hottest bachelor in baseball. Who's going to bag him?"

He rolls his eyes at my recount of the articles printed about him in the last years. "Stalking me on the internet, huh?"

I grin into my beer. "As if you haven't Googled me."

He doesn't deny it and shrugs, going back to drinking his beer in silence.

I look up at the night sky, glad it's still warm out. "So do you just not fuck?"

He nearly chokes on his beer, which makes me laugh as he shakes his head. "Jesus, still no fucking filter on you."

"I told you I wanted to get to know you again, and I'm curious. There has to be a reason the media doesn't know about you being gay."

"Jesus, fuck." He runs his hand through his short blond hair, huffing out a breath in frustration. "Not all of us flaunt our hookups."

I hold the beer bottle by the neck and tip it in his direction. "But if there were any hookups whatsoever, they'd be on it."

He sighs, settling further back into the lounge chair, pulling one arm up to place it behind his head. "NDAs."

My brow crinkles. "You trust them to keep their word because they sign a contract?"

His large shoulder shrugs before he takes another drink of his beer. "I've done my part by having them sign it."

I turn in my chair, studying him for a moment. "What does that mean? Do you want them to out you?"

He doesn't move, his body staying stiff and tense as he looks straight ahead before he finally answers, "I wouldn't say that. But if it happens, it happens. I'm fucking sick of hiding who I am."

My gut hurts, thinking about my best friend living a lie for so long. It's not fucking fair, and he shouldn't have to. "So why not just come out already?"

He scoffs at that like I'm ridiculous. "There's no need. It's nobody's business who I want to fuck."

"Fine, but you shouldn't have to fucking hide."

I watch his jaw tick, and then his already huge chest puffs up and fills with air before he turns to me. "Drop it."

Touchy subject. I get it, but it stings. There was a time I thought nothing was off-limits with us. "Fine."

I turn back in my chair and away from him. He does the same, but he isn't silent. "What about you? Are you really Mr. Commitment now?"

I grin and turn my head in his direction again. "Spying on me too, it seems."

"I may have seen something about you in a long-term relationship. You're really faithful?"

The doubt in his tone pisses me off, but I suppose it's warranted. I've never been committed to anyone in my life. "No, but I have NDAs too."

"That's fucking nice."

I try not to get defensive. The last thing I want is a knockout fight with Ry. The prick has gotten even bigger since the last time either of us has thrown a punch. Most of the time, it was all in good fun, but he could still take my ass out if he wanted to.

"Things with Vicky aren't really as they seem."

"What does that mean?"

I trust Ry, but I can't betray Vicky. "I can't say. But it's pretty much all fake."

He snorts and shakes his head, not looking at all surprised. "Who knew all the shit that came with fame?" He looks up at the sky. "You think if we would have known then what we know now, we would have wasted so much time dreaming about it?"

I hear the raw vulnerability in his voice and feel the pain laced inside the words. "I'm not sure."

I hate this tense moment. I don't really know how to deal with it, so I go all Grady on him and blurt out something completely inappropriate.

"So, you catch or pitch? You know, off the field?"

I caught him off guard, and he turns to me all wide-eyed and freaked-out. "Jesus, fuck. Did you really just ask me that? As if I'm a fucking top or a bottom?"

I shrug my shoulder, having heard those terms before but still thinking it's strange coming from Ry.

Who really is totally fucking gay.

Huh. Who knew?

"I'm just catching up. Is that not an acceptable question?"

He laughs, shaking his head and in the moment, looking like the old Ryan, the one I grew up with. Younger and freer even if he's still all in his head. "Not really. No."

"Oh, come on. I'm just curious, man. I know you're a damn good catcher.

He finishes his beer and places the bottle on the ground. I'm certain he's gonna throw a punch or kick my ass out, but he speaks, "On the field I'm solely a catcher, but off . . ." His eyes meet mine, making me squirm for some unknown reason. "In bed, I like to switch it up."

I gape at him. I have no idea what I thought he was going to say, but the fact that he takes and receives . . . Yeah, I didn't see that coming.

I take a large drink of my beer and lean back in my seat. "I'm sorry you didn't think you could tell me the truth."

"About being versatile in the sack?"

"What?" I turn to him, and it's his turn to laugh at me.

"It's fine, Grady. We were kids. I'm over it."

I don't believe that, but I don't push him. "So, you didn't have sex with anyone in high school?"

"Nope. I was a virgin until my sophomore year of college."

It's on the tip of my tongue to ask him who, but a dark part deep inside keeps me from doing it, and I know it's because I'm not certain I can handle the answer. Thinking about a guy with Ryan, pinning him down and thrusting inside . . .

Okay. That's enough of that.

What the fuck is wrong with me today?

I shake that thought, but it's Ryan who speaks next, answering my unasked question. "My roommate—they put me in the athletic dorms—it was his cousin."

"Wasn't that risky?"

He shrugs. "I was tired of having no experience by that point. My roommate was cool, but I didn't tell him or anyone else. But when his cousin stayed with us a few days, I instantly got a flirty vibe from him. It just sort of happened when Roman went out with the rest of the guys and left us alone."

I hate that his first time was out of desperation. "So, you just jumped the first gay guy you met?"

He punches me in the arm, and I wince but know it wasn't nearly as hard as he could have hit me. "Asshole." He grins. "No. He was good-looking and charming and knew who he was. I was attracted to him."

"Doesn't sound like a love story."

He studies me for an uncomfortable minute but then shrugs his large shoulders. "Nah, but it was decent. Gave me some experience I wanted."

"What about your parents? What do Greg and Cindy say about this?"

He cringes, and my hackles rise. Were they assholes about

it? He recovers, but I can still see the hurt in his eyes. "They um . . ."

"Do they know?"

He nods. "They know. They just ignore it."

I sit up, facing him again. "What do you mean they ignore it?"

"They just keep hoping I'll bring a nice girl home someday." He tries to laugh it off, but it's not fucking funny.

"That's some serious bullshit."

He winces, and I feel like an asshole, but I know I'm not wrong. "It's fine, Grady."

"It's not though. What the fuck is their problem?"

He sits up too, on the edge of his seat, ready to bail. "It could be so much worse. You know where we come from. What they fucking preach relentlessly. They didn't disown me."

"No, they just fucking ignore an entire piece of you."

I watch his throat as his Adam's apple bobs when he swallows, clearly hurt by their bullshit. "Stop." He pins me with a pleading look. "Please."

I nod my head regretfully. "Fine."

He stands up. "You can have free rein of the house. What's mine is yours."

"Like that Everclear song?"

He actually laughs at the memory, of us arguing over who was going to make it and who wasn't, of who would buy the other one a house. I'd always belt out the Everclear song, singing "I will buy you that big house" as loud as I could, which usually resulted in him covering his ears or punching me to shut me up.

"You're a prick."

"Always." I tip the beer in his direction.

"Night, Grady."

"Night, Ryan. Thanks for letting me stay."

He doesn't say anything else as I look around at the not-so-humble results of his fame.

He made it, that's for damn sure.

But at what price?

RYAN

THIS IS INSANITY.

What the hell was I thinking letting him stay here?

I sip my coffee, sitting at the bar in my kitchen, looking out the window as I go over last night. I told him fucking everything. We've been apart for seven years but picked up right where we left off.

Well, minus the kissing.

Fuck me. This is bad.

"Ry, tell me you have coffee." Grady bounces into my kitchen without a care in the world—or clothes.

Motherfucker.

Is he really standing in my kitchen wearing only a pair of tight black briefs?

What the hell is he trying to do to me?

I don't look. I can't look. I point toward the coffee pot with already brewed coffee and look out the window.

"Hell, yeah. You have the good shit."

I roll my eyes but smile into my coffee mug. Same ole Grady.

He walks over to where I am and sits down, his long lanky

legs draped over the stool next to mine. I notice he has tattoos on his muscular thighs. He notices me looking, and I can feel him grinning before I even look up and see it on his ridiculously handsome face. "I went a little ink-crazy."

I shrug, trying hard not to give a fuck. "They aren't bad."

He lifts his right arm, turning to show me his ribcage that has ink scrolled over most of his side. "Nah, most are good, but this one . . ." He points to one that's in messy writing I can barely make out. "This one was supposed to be badass, but it got fucked up."

"A professional did that?"

He chuckles. "I think so, but it wasn't here. I was abroad somewhere. I forgot where."

I study his face and shake my head. "You were drunk."

"Totally."

"What's it supposed to say?" I take the opportunity to study his side but still can't make out the words. My eyes drift over to his smooth stomach. It's defined but not overly so. Flat and toned with a sexy thin trail of dark hair leading south.

I swallow hard, trying to get control of my body as I meet his eyes when he answers my question. "Lyrics. Or they were supposed to be. Really, it's just fucking jibberish." I raise my eyebrow, and he chuckles, "Queen. But they fucked it up. Or I told them wrong. I need to get it fixed."

"Still a Queen fan, huh?"

"Who the fuck isn't?" He grins with an adorable challenge in his eyes that I back down from. Of course, I love the band.

I'm about to profess my love for Queen when my front door bursts open, and I hear heels clicking on my floor.

Goddamn it. Just what I need right now.

"What the fuck?" Grady looks at Jenny in horror as she struts inside.

She looks at him with disgust and then spits venom my way, "What the fuck is a naked Grady Bell doing in your kitchen?"

"I'm not naked." He turns to me. "Who the hell is this?"

I don't get a chance to answer him. "Fine. A mostly naked Grady Bell. Are you trying to give me a coronary?"

"Relax, Jenny." I stand up and place my now-empty coffee mug in the sink, glad I pulled on sweats and a t-shirt before coming to the kitchen. Me being in my underwear too would really set her off.

She holds up her dainty little hand and then looks a little taken aback. "Wait. Grady Bell is gay?"

"I'm not gay." Grady doesn't sound defensive, just setting her straight, but it still does a number on my stupid fucking heart.

"He's not. He's a friend."

Her perfectly manicured eyebrow lifts, studying me. "Fine. Whatever. One crisis at a time."

"Seriously, who the fuck are you?" Grady just can't keep his mouth shut.

She turns to him, not offended but definitely raging. "I'm the best goddamn sports agent in the country."

He turns to me. "You told your agent you're gay?"

I rub my temples with one hand. "If I hadn't, *you* just did."

"Oh, fuck. Sorry." He's not, and it makes me laugh, which annoys me.

"Are you actually laughing?" Jenny studies me, and I think about it. I doubt she's ever heard that sound from me.

"Yeah." I look over at Grady. "And yes, she knows."

"I know," she says, pointing to her chest. "But the world fucking can't."

"That's some real bullshit," Grady grumbles, and again, I smile. How could I ever have thought he wouldn't have my back?

Of course, I think deep down I knew he'd be fine with me being gay—but him not returning the feelings I had for him—yeah, I couldn't handle that shit.

"Quiet, okay? I need to talk to my client." Jesus, Jenny is a fucking ballbuster.

"What's wrong now?" I ask hoping to get the heat off Grady. He didn't hire her. Definitely doesn't deserve her wrath.

"That fucking twink from the other night—he took a picture."

My blood runs cold for a minute as I try to go over the night. But it's Grady's voice I hear next, "I think that's offensive."

I look over at his face, all scrunched up and annoyed and try not to laugh. Jenny ignores him.

"There's no way. He didn't have his phone out. What kind of picture?"

She digs for her phone in her purse and then holds up a pic of me and the cute guy from the other night. We're both fully clothed, outside a bar. Standing near each other, but it's clearly a posed photo.

Grady moves in, examining the photo. "That's your type, huh?"

Not really. I glare at him and then look at Jenny. "It's like every other fan photo I've ever taken. What's the big deal?"

"The big deal is this guy is clearly gay. And you have your arm around him."

"Okay, I know that's offensive. You can't just assume he's gay from a picture." Grady is starting to get pissed, but I don't need or want him fighting my battles for me.

"He's not wrong."

"Look, it doesn't matter. You do not pay me to be politically correct or woke. You pay me to tell you the truth, and the truth is your fan base will assume he's gay. And he is."

Grady moves back to his stool, and I can tell he's stewing but staying quiet.

I shrug, growing tired of her. "So what? It's not like my dick was in his mouth. At least in the pic."

She growls, and Grady chuckles.

She pokes my chest with her bony little finger. "You know your fucking audience. They're about a step up from NASCAR fans. They're God-fearing, beer-drinking, Bible-thumping, country-loving assholes, and they won't like this."

I cringe and want to argue. Obviously, some of my fans are like that but nowhere close to all.

"Oh, come the fuck on. The world is different now. He doesn't need to hide who he is. The world of sports is changing too."

Her eyes narrow in Grady's direction. "Yeah, that's really sweet. And in your rock and roll lifestyle, they'd applaud you for a picture like that. But sports have not changed." She looks at me. "I don't think it will until after you're retired."

"Then maybe I'm in the wrong industry."

I can feel Grady's intense stare on me, but I don't look at him. Jenny softens but only a little and places a hand on my shoulder. "A few more months. They're going to renegotiate that contract. You have to be good. Get the best one you can locked-in. Then you can do pretty much whatever you want."

My stomach actually physically aches, thinking about all this bullshit, but I remain stoic. "Fine. Whatever. It's not like I can take it back now."

"Just be careful." Her eyes glance toward Grady and then back to me. "Really careful."

I hear him snort behind me, but don't care as I lead Jenny toward the front door. I let her out and feel relieved when the door closes behind her.

"She's a cunt."

I turn around to see Grady and grin like a fucking fool. "That's offensive."

He laughs and then punches my shoulder. "What are you doing with an agent like that?"

"She really is the best."

He doesn't seem convinced. "I'm going to go take a shower. Try not to be too offensive while I'm gone."

He laughs, walking toward the kitchen. "Who am I going to offend? You don't even have a fucking house plant."

I laugh but feel a pang of sadness because he's right.

There's not one living thing in my house.

Sometimes I worry I'm not even a living thing these days.

RYAN

Do not touch your dick. Don't fucking do it.

I stare down at my hard-on like it's offending me because it fucking is. The water of my shower sprays my face when I lean into it, hoping to cool off.

I shouldn't be fucking horny right now. I should be horrified. Angry at the world that's so fucked-up that being gay could ruin my career. And that I have a bitchy agent, no matter how good she is at her job.

But no. I'm standing here in cold water, trying to calm my raging boner because my oldest friend—who's straight, by the way—is in my kitchen practically naked.

His body is a work of art. Toned and inked. Lithe and beautiful. Masculine.

And he can just walk around at ease, flaunting it because he has no idea about the fantasies I keep locked deep inside my head.

He thought that kiss between us all those years ago was just good, old-fashioned, drunken fun. And it was for him. Not me.

For me, it was what I've measured every-fucking-thing against since.

First kiss with another guy. Not as good as kissing Grady.

First blow job from another guy. Not as good as kissing Grady.

When I signed with the fucking major leagues.

Not. As. Good. As. Kissing. Grady.

Fuck!

I shut the shower off, climbing out and wrapping a towel around my waist. I jump when I hear Grady's voice booming behind me, "Hey, man. When are you going to give me a tour?"

I turn to look at him, willing my dick to go all the way down because there is no way my fucking towel will hide an erection. "What the fuck are you doing in my bathroom?

He rolls his eyes, walking over to the bathroom counter, lifting his body up and plopping his ass down, making himself at home. "Dude, you practically lived at my house when we were growing up. Do you know how many times I've seen your junk?"

Son of a bitch.

"It's different now," I growl as I turn back toward the mirror, grateful he at least found some fucking sweats. But he's not wearing a shirt, and it's goddamn distracting.

"It's really not. You wasted seven years of friendship, and I'm here to make up for it."

"Why now?" I grab my toothbrush and put some toothpaste on it after asking the question I can't ignore.

"Don't you think it was fate that they practically forced me to sing at the World Series? For the first time. Ever. I mean, I was at the Super Bowl two years ago, but this is the first time I've been invited to the World Series, and it just so happens to be the game you're in."

I raise my toothbrush to my open mouth and start brushing,

contemplating his words. I do think it's a crazy-ass coincidence. I spit in the sink and turn to him, grabbing a towel and wiping my mouth. "So, you just decided to come to my house and demand answers because of fate?"

A slow easy grin spreads across his face. "I've wanted to hunt you down for years. But that was the final push.

"Are you really going to stay for three weeks?"

He chuckles, ignoring my question and hops off my countertop, shocking the holy hell out of me when he drags a finger down the line of my oblique muscles. "Can't believe you have a V, man."

I think about everything nasty I can possibly think of when his nail grazes my muscle, trying to concentrate on his words and not get hard. "What?"

He chuckles and pulls his hand away. "How many hours do you spend in the gym a day? There's no way I could ever have that much discipline."

My eyes drag slowly over his torso, noting that he has a V himself pointing deliciously below the waist of his sweats, but it's just not nearly as prominent as mine. "I'd say you're doing just fine."

He winks, and it makes my stupid heart flutter.

Fuck. Fuck. Fuck.

I step away from him and go into my room. Of course, the fucker follows me. I grab a pair of boxer briefs and slip them on under the towel which makes him chuckle again as he takes a seat on my bed.

"No, please. Make yourself at home."

"I will."

I roll my eyes and grab a pair of jeans, pulling them on and tossing the towel in the hamper. I grab a t-shirt and tug it on over my head before turning to face him. "You going to take a shower today? Or at least put on a shirt?"

He stands up and wraps an arm around my shoulder. "Always in your head, Ry. Show me around this bigass mansion."

"You seriously need a tour?"

"Yup." I grumble my way through the upstairs and main level because he's a persistent fucker, and I know I'll have to show him every single room before we finally get down to the basement where I spend most of my time.

"Damn, man." He whistles in appreciation, and I laugh at his ridiculousness. "This is fancy as shit."

"Right, like you don't have a bigass, fancy house in California."

He grins all-knowingly. "You really have been stalking me."

I may have seen something on one of those gossip "news" shows a time or two about his California mansion. "Whatever." I point to my left. "That's the gym."

"Makes sense." He eyes my body, and I try like hell not to squirm. He's got to quit that shit.

"Yeah, um . . ." We walk further into the basement. "This is the home theater."

"Nice. I have a bowling alley in mine."

Competitive fucker. "And how often do you bowl?"

He laughs at that, carefree and easy. "Never."

I dismiss him and then stop short before we head into the next room. But, of course, he pushes past me and into the room.

"Holy. Shit. Bailey." I walk inside reluctantly.

"What?"

"A music room? You can't carry a tune, and you have a music room?" He looks around the room in awe. It has several guitars, a piano, and various other instruments. Some signed records that were sent as gifts over the years.

He walks over to one guitar and instantly throws the strap over his shoulder. Why?"

"Why what?" I play dumb.

"Why what?" He looks down at the guitar that's never been played. "This is nicer than my collection."

"Bullshit." I take a seat on the small sofa in the middle of the room. "It's not a big deal."

"Were you waiting for me, Bailey?"

I look away, and my eyes roll, trying to show indifference. But when he takes a seat next to me, his long fingers seeking out the chords of the guitar and bringing it to life, I almost stop breathing.

It's been so damn long since I've been next to him while he's played. I recognize the song instantly and look him dead in the eye.

"Really? Elton John?"

"Hey 'Your Song' is a brilliant fucking song. It's a classic."

I shake my head. He's always loved the classics. "You know anything from this decade?"

He laughs, but then turns serious as the notes change, and my blood runs cold because I know this song too.

Immoral.

His voice fills the air, and chills run up my arms.

"I'm drowning." He strums the guitar, his silky voice just as perfect as I remember it.

"I'm sinking." *I can't hear this song right now.*

"Can't stop shivering." My eyes lock on his as he plays, still singing his own song. A song I know he wrote.

"They love me. I'm their fantasy."

Fuck.

"But they can't see me. They just don't know." His eyes remain on me, and there's a deep sadness in them. "Even I don't wanna be me."

"Goddamn it, Grady." I stand up, and he stops playing.

"Not a fan?"

I turn around to face him. "Of my best friend feeling like he's drowning? No. I'm not."

"It won a Grammy."

He's trying to play it off, but every time I hear that song, recorded or live, I feel the pain residing in the words. "It's fucking depressing."

"So is your sour-ass mood." He lifts the strap of the guitar off his shoulders and lays the guitar down. His hand runs through his thick black hair. "It's just a song."

"You wrote it though?"

He confirms with a nod. "I was in a pissy mood."

Which is rare for him. Or it was before. "I'm sorry."

For a minute, I think he's going to stay serious, but that's just not Grady. Instead, he shoves my arm and then stands up, looking around. "We should throw a party."

"What?" I stare up at him in a daze.

"A party. You just won the motherfucking World Series. You need to celebrate."

"No."

"Yes."

He walks out of the room with a determined smile, and I lean my head back against the sofa.

I guess we're having a party.

GRADY

Earlier in the music room, things got way too heavy. I can't handle that shit, so I do what I do best . . . I threw a party. Gathering people to celebrate my best friend's win.

I look around at the back patio and smile because it wasn't hard to find people to celebrate with Ry, even if he probably didn't think he had this many people in his corner.

He likes to pretend he's a loner, but the truth is, people are drawn to Ryan. They just are. He's always had this allure. He thought it was because of me. It wasn't. People have always liked him. Girls thought he was shy, and they wanted to be the one to break him out of his shell. Guys saw him as loyal. And I imagine it's the same now.

Even though he's not interested in the chicks, I see they still flock to him. He's currently bombarded by three chicks who came with one of his teammates. I think they may be his wife's friends, but I can't be too sure.

The party is stacked with people.

I watch with a grin as one of the chicks continues to waste her perfect rack on him, leaning in and giving him a glimpse of ample cleavage. Flipping her long blond hair and giggling at everything he says. I realize it's totally lost on him.

I chuckle at that thought, and Waylon, who's standing right next to me, eyes me with curiosity. "What's so funny?"

I haven't told him about Ryan being gay. It's not my place, and I won't betray his trust. "Nothing."

"Seems like your friend is going to get lucky tonight." He sips his fruity drink, oblivious to Ryan's secret like everyone else here.

I turn back to look at Ry and how uncomfortable he seems with the blonde's attention, but I think it could easily be misconstrued as him being shy. It's unbelievable to me that he's had to hide who he really is all these years.

I look around the party that's mostly full of baseball players, their wives or girlfriends, and their friends. I don't see one gay couple here. Seemingly the only two gay guys here are Waylon and Ryan, and I wonder if he was able to be himself—if he were out and proud—would the party be different?

Would he have other gay friends or people here that he might actually want to fuck?

He must sense my thoughts on him because his eyes meet mine. He offers me a small smile and shakes his head before going back to his conversation with the chick who has no chance.

He deserves that. A party where he can tell the chick to keep her stupid small hand off his shoulder and go and flirt with a dude. He deserves to take as many pictures as he wants with whoever the fuck he wants to and invite whoever he wants to his own party.

The list he gave me was all his teammates. No one else.

I think about the song I played for him this morning. The song I wrote two years ago after a drunken, lonely night. I had been at a club, dancing with an insanely hot chick, but my mind went to him.

I have no idea why, and I've never talked about the song's meaning out in public. Always letting it be a mystery, but I went home alone that night. Climbed into my bed and drifted off to sleep only to wake up, gasping for air and feeling like I was drowning. My bad boy image. Letting women think they could be the one to tame me.

I'm their fantasy.

But they don't know me.

I take a drink of the margarita Waylon forced on me and cringe. *Why do people add sugary shit to alcohol? Give me straight tequila any fucking day.*

"Who's that?" My thoughts are interrupted by Waylon's question, and I look to see who he's talking about.

A guy walks over toward Ry and swings his lanky arm around him, and I realize I'm gripping my drink a little too tight as I watch them, nearly crushing the plastic cup. "Bennett Rochet. Pitcher."

Waylon stares at them alongside me. "They seem chummy."

I have no idea why the sight of them laughing and talking with that fucker's arm still around Ry's shoulder makes me feel uneasy, but I think my voice sounds semi-normal when I shrug and say, "They're friends."

"Aw," Waylon turns to me with a smile filled with shit-eating fuckery on his face. "Does your old bestie have a new bestie?"

"Fuck off," I growl a little too seriously and then shake my head, laughing when Waylon feigns hurt, clutching his chest.

"Don't be jealous."

"I'm not jealous." I know he means it in a friends sense. I *know* that, but something just feels fucking off about the whole damn thing, and I get defensive.

"Alright, sweetie. Why don't you get introduced, huh? I'm sure Bennett will share."

"Ry" nearly comes out of my mouth, and I check myself just in time. "Sure."

We walk over, and I nod toward Ryan in a greeting that feels stiff and awkward. "You gonna introduce us to our newest guest?"

Ry laughs. "You know this is still only my house, right, fucker?"

The girls giggle, and the guy—Bennett—laughs but finally releases Ry and holds his hand out for me. "Bennett Rochet, and you're Grady fucking Bell from Immoral." He nudges Ry. "Bailey didn't tell me he knew Grady Bell. My wife is going to kill him."

Bailey. Motherfucker. That's my nickname for him. I'm the only one that gets to call him that. I grip his hand a little too tightly and try to keep my voice neutral. "Why's that?"

He grins as our hands disconnect and drop to our sides. "She's a huge fan, man. Huge. And she skipped the party today. She's going to be pissed."

Right. He's married. With a kid on the way. The dude is straight.

Why that matters, I have no idea. But when that fact comes back into light, I relax a little. "You want me to sign something?"

Ryan shakes his head and takes a drink from his red plastic cup. "Unbelievable."

I eye him. "What? I can't help that I have fans everywhere."

Bennett just nods his head. "I'm definitely getting your autograph. It's either that or pretend like none of this happened, and I'm pretty sure there are photographers hanging around outside."

Waylon clears his throat next to me, getting pissy. "Are you going to introduce me or am I going to stand here like pretty little furniture all night?"

Ryan chuckles, his eyes zoning in on Waylon, and I wonder for a moment if Waylon is his type. I mean, he looks pretty damn similar to the guy Jenny was freaking out about, the one Ryan definitely did hook up with.

"Um yeah, sorry. This is my manager, Waylon." Most of the girls have moved along, leaving only Bennett, Ryan, Waylon, and me, so I turn to Ry next. "Waylon, this is Ryan Bailey." Then to Bennett. "And Bennett Rochet, who I just met too."

They both wave at him, and I think Waylon might be drooling when Ryan shakes his hand. "Well, it's nice to meet you boys." He shakes Bennett's hand, but his eyes go right back to Ry. *What the fuck? Is he interested in him? Does Waylon know Ryan's gay?*

I shake the thought away, pretty fucking sure I'm bordering on offensive right now.

"I can't believe Grady didn't tell me his best friend from high school is Ryan Bailey."

"You follow baseball?" Ryan asks, not in a surprised tone. No, it's more like getting-to-know-you fucking talk, and it irks me for some strange reason.

"No," Waylon laughs. "Not big on sports, but I have seen you featured on some of my favorite shows and sites." Waylon winks, actually fucking winks, and Ry, I swear to you, blushes.

Fuck.

What if they're into each other?

My body tenses. *Why the hell do I care? Waylon is a good guy. Why should I care if my friends are into each other?*

Shit, I'm really losing it.

"You okay?" Ryan's eyes are boring into me, concern dripping from his features.

I nod and try to brush it off, playing it cool. "I'm fine." I turn to Bennett. "So, you're the pitcher to Ry's catcher, huh?"

Ryan, who unfortunately had just taken a drink, nearly chokes and sputters, "Did you seriously just fucking ask that?"

Bennett looks confused, his eyebrows pinching together. "What? I *am* a pitcher."

Ryan clears his throat, pounding on his chest once and then catches his breath. "Yeah, I know." He tries to play it cool as his glare moves to me. "He knows that too."

Waylon giggles next to me, taking another drink, but I don't think he picked up on my double entendre, which okay—it was an asshole question to ask after my talk with Ry about pitching and catching.

Bennett tosses out a question my way. "You play?"

"I did. I used to be the *pitcher* for Ry." *Why did I emphasize that word?*

I feel Ry's eyes on me, trying to pierce through the bullshit and let me know how pissed he is, but I just smile at Bennett, who laughs. "Holy shit, he never told me that either. We should all hang out and play sometime."

I raise my hands and shake my head. "Oh, no way. I'm not up to playing with the big boys these days. I'm all about music now."

He laughs, but Ryan looks like he wants to murder me and like I've lost my mind.

Yeah well, he's not the only one that's confused by my behavior tonight.

What the hell is going on with me?

RYAN

"OKAY, what the hell was all that about?"

"What do you mean?" Grady is trying to play dumb. I can feel it as he helps me clean up the mess left by all the party guests he invited. But I'm not letting him off the hook.

"You know what I mean, asshole. What the fuck was that?"

He tosses a beer bottle into the trash and plops down on the outdoor sofa by the firepit. "I don't know."

I move to sit next to him. "What do you mean you don't know? The way you questioned Bennett? I mean what the fuck was that? Catcher and pitcher? Seriously?"

I nearly choked when he asked Bennett—my very, very straight teammate—if he was the pitcher to my catcher. Bennett may not have picked up on the double meaning, but I know that's the way Grady meant it.

Grady, always calm, cool, and collected, looks freaked the fuck out as he runs his fingers through his thick black hair.

"Grady, what's up?"

His green eyes lock on mine, and I feel a tremor through my body. "I don't know. I'm sorry. I just . . ." He looks away and sighs, "I saw you and Bennett together and how close you two are . . ."

"We're teammates. And friends."

"Nothing more?" His eyes meet mine again, and I can see he's serious.

"No. *Jesus.*" I stare at him in confusion. "He's straight." I grow irrationally irritated with his question. "And *married*. With a kid on the way."

He drops his hand from his hair and shrugs. "It's been known to happen before."

"Not with me. I don't fuck around with straight guys." *Not after him for damn sure.* "And especially *married*, straight guys. What kind of person do you think I am?"

"What about Waylon?"

I search his expression. *Is he fucking with me?* "What about Waylon?"

His shoulder lifts, but he doesn't pull off the nonchalance. Not at all. "He's gay."

"So?"

"So . . ." He's running his fucking fingers through his hair again, and I don't like how tense he looks. "Is he your type?" I laugh, the sound escaping and making him scowl at me. "What? He's gay and good-looking.

"Right. And I only have two requirements. Quit being such an asshole." I stand up, annoyed with this conversation.

"I'm not being an asshole." I turn back to look at him, and he looks . . . Confused? Upset? I'm not really sure. But the need to comfort him is there. I don't think he's trying to be an asshole. I think he's trying to figure something out.

"He's not really my type."

I sit down next to him again, and he turns to face me. "He's exactly the same type as the guy you were with. The one that Jenny was all cunty about."

I lean back against the sofa and groan, "He was cute. And Waylon is too, but that's not exactly my type, not usually anyway."

I can feel him studying me intently, and I don't fucking like it. It makes me feel vulnerable and exposed. Two things I never want to be. "So, what *is* your type?"

I groan, lifting my hands up to cover my face. I can't say him. That Grady Bell is my ultimate type. I drop my hands and turn my head to look at him. "I usually like bigger guys."

"Like chubby? I've heard that's a thing."

"Oh my God," I groan again, but it turns into a laugh as I try to be patient with him. "No. Not really. Just, not a hundred pounds soaking wet. I like bigger guys. Strong muscles. Guys who can keep up and who I'm not afraid I'm going to hurt."

I can't quite make out the expression on his face right now, and maybe it's the drinks I had today, but I swear I see a flicker of fire in those eyes. Dangerous fire that has to be my mind playing tricks on me.

"Oh."

His eyes slowly drag down over my chest and then back up. "So, someone like you?"

Christ. "I don't know. Not necessarily my size. Just . . ." *Do not say his body is fucking perfect. That he's fucking perfect.* "Not small."

He studies me again, his eyes searching mine. "Do you ever think about that night?"

He's not doing this right now. "How much have you had to drink?"

"Not much. It was mostly fruity drinks anyway, and they've worn off. Stop changing the subject and answer the question."

"What does it matter?" I stand up, angry that he'd do this to me. As if I haven't been tortured enough.

"It matters." He stands too, and he's close, too close. I back up toward the house because my chest is tightening, and I can't catch my breath.

"It doesn't. None of it matters." He stalks me, his lithe body quickly caging me against the side of the house and him. All fucking him.

"It matters. Tell me."

"No. It doesn't." He raises his hands, placing them on either side of my head, surveying my face. "You're straight."

"So?"

"So?" The question sounds so fucking ridiculous. "You're straight. I'm not. I'm a fucking guy, and you're looking at me like . . . like . . ."

He leans in closer, almost predatorily, and I think my lungs might actually burst from trying to take in air. "Like what?"

My eyes involuntarily dip to his mouth, his full, pink lips. "Like you want another taste."

A growl erupts from his throat as his hand hooks behind my neck, and he tugs my mouth to his before I have a chance to argue or move away, not that I could if I even fucking tried. As his lips collide with my own, I'm right fucking back there.

To that first and only time we kissed. To that feeling of being whole for the first time in my life.

Of wanting and desire that's both crippling and breathing the life back into me.

His lips seal against mine as his hand grips the back of my neck, holding me there as he kisses me, exploring. When I feel his tongue run over the seam of my mouth, I open, knowing I shouldn't let him in but unable to deny him.

His moan hits my ears when I give him access to my mouth, and I groan when his large body presses against mine, his cock hard and grinding against my own solid length. "Grady," I try, but he ignores me.

His mouth is assaulting mine, and God help me, I love it. I can't catch my breath, but I don't want to. My hands move to his hips, and I yank him even closer to me as the kiss intensifies. Then I just lean into it, for once granting myself something I actually want.

Something I've wanted for so goddamn long.

His hand moves in my hair and digs in, grabbing hold and tugging my head back to look into my eyes.

I expect shame or regret, but it's all lust and fire. His hands drop to the hem of my shirt and lift. "This. Off."

We're moving way too fast. I should stop this, but I can't. Because I don't want to. Instead, I lift my arms and let him remove my shirt, tossing it behind us somewhere. His eyes drift over my torso, taking his time. He's not rushing anything. It's slow and methodical, taking in every inch of my skin visible in the full moon and lights from the pool.

"You're fucking art." His eyes meet mine, and I realize it's genuine. Brutal, frank honesty that continues to steal my breath.

"What's happening here?"

The right side of his mouth pulls up in a sexy, confident grin. "Whatever we want to."

"You're . . ." He places a finger on my lips that are slightly swollen and tingling from his kiss and shakes his head.

"Don't." He drops his hand to the waist of my jeans and pulls me to him as his mouth meets mine again. "I'm Bell." He kisses me softly. "You're Bailey." His hands thread through my hair, and that's it.

No more fighting it.

At least for right now. I know this is a stupid mistake. I know, deep down, he's going to regret this tomorrow, or I will. Either way, it'll be labeled as an error in judgment, but right now, I can't bring myself to care.

Not with the way his hips are grinding his cock against mine and how his hands are trailing over my chest, making sure to hit every single dip and groove of muscle.

I reach for his shirt, wanting to feel his skin against mine, and he doesn't fight me, only grumbling at the loss of contact as I lift his shirt over his head, and then we reconnect. His skin is warm and damp with sweat, like my own, and it feels so goddamn good. A needy groan escapes my mouth, and he swallows it with his own.

We're desperate for each other. My balls ache with the need to come, and I can't believe how close I am. I wonder if he's feeling the same way, and with the way he clings to me, his mouth unwavering, I'd say he is.

God, he feels good. He's nearly my height, strong and confident as his hands roam over my body. We press together with our tongues exploring every inch of each other's mouth.

It's too much. It's all too damn much. And when his hand moves to the button on my jeans, I finally regain my wits.

"Grady. Don't."

"What's the matter, Ry?" He's as breathless as I am, his eyes clouded with lust as they meet mine. "Don't be shy."

"I'm not fucking shy." My hand clasps his wrist, and my

heart sinks because I don't know what this is, but I know it's not real. "But we can't do this."

He smiles, but it doesn't reach those beautiful eyes of his. It's nervous and unsure. "But we are."

I shake my head and push his body backward, releasing his wrist. "We aren't. We should go to sleep." I head for the patio door, unable to look at him. "We can finish cleaning up tomorrow."

"Ry." I hear his strangled plea, but I ignore it, opening the door and slipping inside my house before I lose control.

I can't do this.

We cannot do this.

GRADY

I DON'T WANT to get up and face the day, not even a little bit. I kissed him. I more than kissed him.

And he pushed me away.

Yet again.

All night, I went over the moments of last night. His hands, large and commanding. His lips were soft but firm. The way I remember them. His body is all hard edges and brute strength. But still, I was able to hold him there against the outside of the house, demanding his attention.

Until I wasn't.

Until he walked away from me yet again.

I have no idea what that kiss meant. I've never been attracted to another guy in my entire life, but with Ry, it's different. Neither time was just a drunken fluke. I wanted it. Both times.

But it has to be clear to my stupid fucking brain by now that he just doesn't want me.

I mean, he's gay. He isn't struggling with his sexuality, so it isn't that, like I thought it was in high school. No. It has to be me.

Fucking great.

I finally sit up in the bed in one of his guest rooms and grab my phone off the side table. I see a text from Waylon, asking if we can get together and tell him I'm still at Ryan's.

He tells me he's on his way, and I cringe, thinking maybe I should have asked Ryan first. I mean, I don't fucking know. What's the protocol for the day after you blow someone off? Does he even want to see me? Does he need space? Is it cool for me to just invite my manager over?

Fuck. I've never worried about anything this much in my life.

I grumble as I stand up, tugging on a pair of sweatpants because I'm pretty sure only briefs is a no-no at this point.

I walk down to the kitchen and see Ryan is already there, dressed in shorts and a cutoff shirt. "Going somewhere?"

His stormy blue eyes meet mine, and I see the concern written all over his face. "For a run."

I nod my head at that, never having felt as fucking awkward as I do right now. Not because I kissed a guy, but because said guy pushed me away.

"Okay, um . . . Waylon needs to talk about something with me and is on his way over." I drag my hand through my hair awkwardly. "Is that okay?"

"The dude who was here just yesterday?" His tone screams annoyance, and I walk a little closer to him, annoyed by him being annoyed.

"Yeah. My manager. I just didn't know if you were kicking my ass out this morning or not."

His shitty attitude seems to deflate at least a little. "Of course, I'm not."

"You sure about that, Ry? You looked ready to pack up and bolt from your own house last night."

He sighs and walks even closer to me now, his eyes scanning my face, and I think for a minute he might touch me. Maybe even kiss me, but he takes a step back. "I'm not running. And I'm not kicking you out. But what happened last night . . .

I fill the gap he just put between our bodies, my bare toes touching his tennis shoes. "A hot as fuck kiss."

I watch his Adam's apple bob erratically in his throat and notice he looks pained. "It can't happen again, Grady."

"What? Why not?" I may not have any experience with guys, but I know I liked having this one in particular pressed against me last night.

He looks at me like I'm stupid. "You like girls."

My hand moves to his hip, wanting to pull him closer, but he's a big fucker, and especially when he's tense like this, he's not moving. "I like one guy."

"No." He shakes his head and pushes my hand away. "Look, maybe you like both, and if you do, you should go for it. You should go and kiss a whole bunch of boys, but not me."

"Why the hell not?" It stings. I hate that it fucking stings, but I think I need to hear him say it, say he just isn't into me. Maybe he really is into the smaller guys. Softer, I don't know. And if that's true, that's fine, but I want to hear it.

"Because I'm not going to be your fucking experiment, Grady. I'm just not. So, yeah. No more kissing."

He starts toward the front door, and I want to fucking chase after him, but I don't know what to say to that. I hear the front door click and shortly after, I buzz Waylon in who's frantic by the time he gets to the front door. "Okay, so I have a great opportunity for you."

"Hey to you too," I say, and he waves me off, taking a seat on the couch in Ryan's living room.

"Hey. I have a great . . ." His face drops as I plop down next to him. "What's the matter?"

"What? Nothing?"

He studies me, clearly not buying it. "No." He waves his hand in my direction. "Something is definitely wrong. You look like someone died." He clutches his chest. "Did someone die?"

"No," I laugh because he cracks me up even when I feel like shit. "Something kind of happened."

"What?" He leans forward, interested now.

I take a deep breath. "I kissed Ry."

His nose scrunches up. "Ry? As in Ryan Bailey?"

"Yup." I slouch back into the comfy cushion behind me. "That one."

"Oh my God. Wait, what?" He looks shocked, and I guess it could be a shock. Ryan isn't even out, and I'm supposedly straight.

"Once on graduation night and then again last night."

"Wow." His eyes are wide, and it would be comical if, again, I didn't feel like total shit right now.

"Yeah."

"So . . . I mean what happened? And who the hell kissed who?"

"I kissed him." I shrug. "Both times. But he kissed me back."

He's processing, his back straight and his hands on his knees as he goes over the information I just gave him. "So, who is the one freaking out? You or him? Or both?"

My fingers rake through my hair, and at this point I'm surprised I have any left. "Look," I meet his eyes. "You can't say anything, but Ryan . . ." I look toward the door as if he's going to walk through, and then back at Waylon, who is as much a friend as he is my manager. "He's not exactly straight."

His lips purse together. "I thought maybe I got a vibe yesterday but wasn't sure."

I nearly growl at his words, thinking about what the hell that could mean but decide to keep on going instead of investigating this "vibe." "Right.

"So, it's you that's freaking out?"

"No." I shake my head. "He did. Both fucking times. He ran, not me."

"But you're straight?" He says it like a question, and I shrug.

"I don't fucking know. All I know is I really, really liked kissing him both times."

He gapes at me, his eyes wide and his jaw dropped before his puts a hand on my shoulder. "Oh, honey, You love him, huh?"

An uncomfortable feeling swirls deep in my gut. A feeling I've pushed away for so damn long and never let myself get close to again.

"We're friends."

"Right. *Friends*." He nods his head, but it's condescending like he doesn't believe me at all. "You know, one time I got really drunk and ended up kissing one of my best friends. He was great, and I mean drop-dead gorgeous. I should have loved kissing him." I turn to focus on him, wondering where he's going with this. "Anyway, halfway into the kiss, we both stopped and just started cracking up. I mean, it was like kissing my brother. And he felt the exact same. We never did it again."

Yeah, kissing Ry is definitely not like kissing a brother. It was fucking hot. My body actually heats up and tingles just thinking about it. I clear my throat and try to push the memories away. "Yeah, it wasn't like that with him. It was hot."

He pats me again on the shoulder, smiling. "I think you're in love, my friend. Like actual love."

"He can't seem to get over the fact that I've never been with a guy before."

He gnaws on his bottom lip, thinking about that information, no-doubt. "Aren't you freaking out about that a little?"

I smile and shrug. "Maybe a little. But I don't know . . . You know me, Waylon. I go with the flow."

He offers me a megawatt smile of his own. "So, the fact that he has a dick and not a . . ." his face actually scrunches up in disgust, "vagina . . ." He shudders, and fuck, I do too, hearing him say the word.

"Don't ever say that again."

He holds up one hand in the air. "That I can promise." We both laugh, and then he moves on. "It really doesn't bother you?"

I've never really thought about my sexuality before. I've just been with whoever I've been attracted to at the time, and it just so happens, it was usually women, except Ry. "No. Not when it comes to him. I want him."

"Be sure. Completely sure. And then go for it, if that's what you want. Confidence is sexy, my friend. No matter what gender you're working with."

"Thanks, Waylon."

"Anytime." When he straightens his back again, I know he's about to get down to business. "Okay, so now we need to get to me and this charity I booked for you. And you have to do it."

I laugh, grateful I have him in my life.

But so damn afraid even with him to lean on, I'm going to fuck it all up.

Or even worse, that Ry isn't into me at all.

RYAN

AFTER MY RUN, I snuck in the side door, hoping to avoid Grady and Waylon. I can't seem to deal today. My mind is planted firmly on that kiss with Grady last night. What the fuck was I thinking?

And why did I stop it?

I strip out of my damp clothes and climb into my shower, trying like hell to shake that thought from my head. I know why I stopped it.

He's. Not. Gay.

It would be so damn easy to give in to the fantasy. To kiss him and touch him, all the while pretending it wouldn't have an expiration date. And a quick one at that. But I can't do it.

I'm not a dumbass kid who thinks a kiss with me could change who he is. I turn the water a little cooler, hoping like hell it will tame the raging hard-on I've had since his lips touched mine last night.

I turn off the shower, frustrated and angry with so many things. I see my phone flashing with notifications as I get dressed, but I ignore it. I don't want to hear about PR opportunities and obligations. I don't want to check in with my mother about everything that doesn't make her uncomfortable.

Everything that rides on the right side of her fantasy life.

I'm drowning.

I'm sinking.

Can't stop sinking.

The words to Immoral's song run over and over in my head.

They love me.

I'm their fantasy.

But they can't see.

Even I don't wanna be me.

"Fuck." I stare into the mirror as I pull on a plain tee and jeans before reaching for a baseball hat and planting it on my head, pulling it low, shielding my eyes because I can't even look at myself.

Living a lie. Every single day to appease everyone else.

I grab a pair of sunglasses and pull them on to help with that pesky reflection even more. When I make it out the front door, I see Waylon and Grady standing by the fancy sports car that was parked here when I got back.

I can't avoid him forever. I give a quick wave, and Waylon offers a bright smile that can't be fake. The guy is all sunshine and happiness, and it's almost, almost contagious. "Well, hello again."

"Hi, Waylon." I make my way over to them, looking at Waylon even though my shades are dark, and I'm not sure anyone can tell where I'm looking, "I was just going to grab some coffee. You guys want to join me?"

Please say no.

Waylon smiles and pats my shoulder. "I'd love to, but I have a plane to catch." He turns to Grady, wrapping an arm around his shoulder. "But Grady here could use a pick-me-up."

Grady looks tense as hell, and I'm not sure what to do with that. He's always completely carefree. "Yeah. I'll go." Shit. He turns to Waylon and hugs him properly. "Be good, you little shit."

"Aw, don't you worry about me." He blows him a kiss and winks at me before climbing into his car and driving away.

I turn to Grady. "You don't have to go if you don't want to."

"I want to." His green eyes are locked on mine with the same intensity as last night and this morning, and I turn toward the garage.

"Okay. Let's go."

He follows me into the garage, and we climb into my truck. He looks around the cab and then back at me. "Seriously? A pickup truck?"

I shrug. "What?"

"You really are trying to make sure they don't see, huh?"

I roll my eyes and back out of the garage. "Gay men can drive trucks. Jesus."

He laughs, "I'm just saying."

I exit my gate and head toward my favorite coffee shop. "It's a perk. It was given to me for being in a commercial. I'm a fucking sellout."

He chuckles at that and then cocks his head to the side. "Well, fuck. I've never gotten a vehicle. Cash, yeah. Vodka." I grin thinking about the top shelf vodka ads he's been in throughout the years. "Never anything with a motor."

"Guess you're just going to have to try harder."

He relaxes back into his seat, and I feel a little tension release from my shoulders as we joke around about all the ways we've sold out over the years, and then I finally pull into park at the coffee place.

I leave my sunglasses in the car but keep the hat on as we walk inside. I smile when I see Justin is working. He shoots me a great big smile. "I was wondering if I'd see you today. Congrats on winning the World Series!"

I grin. "Thanks. I thought you weren't a fan." He's worked here for two years, and I come in often, so we have our own little routine.

"Oh, I'm not a *baseball* fan." He winks, and I smile at that.

"Well, thanks for the support." His brown eyes are almost shimmering with gold flecks. "I'll take my usual."

"Of course." He looks nervously over my shoulder. "Wow. You're Grady Bell."

"Yeah, I'm here." I hear Grady's voice, but it barely sounds like him with a clipped tone, lacking all his usual charm.

"What can I get you, Mr. Bell?"

"Coffee. Black."

Justin looks at me, a flirty smile on his handsome face. "Hmmm, plain black coffee for the rockstar."

I smile at that as Justin begins working, and I feel Grady tense as all hell at my side. "What the fuck does that mean?"

"What does *what* mean?" I turn to look at him, seeing the grim look on his face.

"Plain coffee? Like I'm fucking boring or something."

I stare at him, my right eyebrow lifted in confusion. "I don't think he meant anything by it." I keep my voice low, not wanting anyone to hear.

"I can switch it up too, Ry."

"What the hell is your problem?"

He doesn't answer me, and I count myself lucky because

Justin arrives with my lowfat mocha. "I added a little more mocha this time. I think you deserve a little extra."

"Thanks, I appreciate it."

"Plain, black coffee." He holds out a cup to Grady who takes it, but I can tell he's still pissy as hell.

Before Grady can say anything else, I pay, leaving a large tip and guide Grady outside toward my truck. "What the hell is your problem?"

He turns angrily toward me. "What's my problem?" He covers his heart with his free hand. "I thought you weren't out."

I think about his words for a minute and look around at the parking lot that's pretty damn full with people walking in and out of the coffee place. "I told you I fucking am. Lower your voice," I say, keeping my voice low.

"Right. You're fucking out, but I have to keep quiet about it, and so do you. And your fucking agent."

"What's your point?" I hiss.

"You know what my point is? What the hell was that in there with him?" He points toward the coffee shop.

"With Justin? The barista? It was a fucking coffee order that I make almost every day."

"Are you fucking him?"

I wince at his question and instinctively look around the parking lot, glad I don't see anyone nearby. I grab his arm and pull him closer but keep a distance between our bodies. "Careful. You sound like a jealous fucking boyfriend right now."

He takes another step closer to me, tipping his chin up with no shame. "Maybe I fucking am."

"Stop," I order, my heart racing as a group of young women walk out the door with coffees in hand, their eyes on Grady and me and their cell phones out, not at all inconspicuously taking pictures of us. I release my hold on him but look him in the eye. "Stop."

"Ry . . ." He doesn't get to finish whatever he was going to say because a car pulls up and then another, both parking near us with photographers rushing out and clicking photos. "Fuck." He turns to me. "Since when does KC have paparazzi?"

I shrug. "Since my team won the world series and Grady fucking Bell is in town. Come on." I unlock my truck and wave at the cameras, giving them one good shot, ignoring their questions about what we're doing here together and climb into my truck.

Grady tells them he's happy to be back home and flashes a peace sign before climbing in the passenger side. I see them rushing to get back in their cars and follow us as I drive leisurely back to my house. I have a gate that keeps everyone out and far from the front door of my house so I'm not really worried.

My house is public record. They already know where I live.

"A fucking peace sign? Really?"

He chuckles, and it's good to hear. "Fuck off. I'm supposed to be more family-friendly these days."

"And why is that?" I know Victoria, the woman he's supposedly dating is on a family show, but he's a rockstar. Does anyone really expect him to be a good boy?

He shrugs, and his expression darkens. "I do what the label tells me to do."

I recognize that anguish, doing what you have to for everyone else. But I don't commiserate with him out loud. There's no point.

We both know we're both stuck in our own hell, although he plays it off a hell of a lot better.

GRADY

I NEED to get my shit together.

I know that. I'm fucking losing it.

After coffee, Ry headed downstairs to his home gym to work out, and I went for a swim, hoping to release some of my tension. This isn't me.

Tense. Angry. Brooding. Jealous.

None of those things describe me.

But I feel like I can't fucking breathe. Seeing that fucker grin and wink at Ryan at the coffee shop and Ry actually fucking flirting back? Yeah, that shit set me off.

Because maybe I'm not his fucking type. Maybe that bullshit about a bigger, more solid guy was all bullshit. Justin was thin with a hint of muscle but nowhere near my build. And not even close to Ryan's.

And then, Justin's little shot at me getting plain coffee. Like I'm just a boring straight guy? Fuck him.

I pull myself out of the pool and dry off, wrapping the towel around my shoulders and walk inside.

Waylon said to be sure. Well, I'm fucking sure. I don't want Ryan fucking any baristas. Or managers. Or anyone else. That thought alone makes my stomach turn and my heart clench tightly in my chest.

But I need to be confident.

Something I've never had a hard time with before.

I walk into the gym and see Ry, stopping short at the entrance and in a fucking trance as I watch him lift weights, cultivating every single muscle on his body. He's only wearing a pair of black shorts.

His skin is glistening with sweat, and I can see he has earbuds in so I take this moment to watch him. He lifts a weight, curling it and making every muscle in his arm and shoulders flex. His abs are fucking shredded and ripple with each movement.

I've been able to admit when a man is good-looking before, but none of them have ever made my mouth fucking water. Ry though, holy fuck. I'm stunned stupid by each bicep curl as he slowly lifts the heavy weight up and then down.

He's beautiful.

Everything about him is fucking beautiful. And I have no idea what it means for my sexuality, but I don't care. I know I'm attracted to him, and I'm not afraid to explore that.

"Ry." He doesn't hear me, but he places the weights down and then turns, startling when he sees me.

"Fuck." He rips his earbuds out. "What are you doing in here?"

"What?" I stride into the gym. "I'm not allowed to use your fancy gym?"

He's still in a pissy mood from earlier, which I expected. "I told you my house is your house."

"Right." I walk closer to him, ignoring his obvious apprehension at my close proximity. "You look good."

I watch in awe as his throat flexes. He swallows tightly, and I can see the nerves there. "Grady . . ."

I hold up a hand, halting his words. "I was fucking jealous today."

"Don't—"

I cut him off. Confidence is sexy. "I was. I hated seeing that guy flirting openly with you. I fucking hated it. Hell, I think I was jealous of both Bennett *and* Waylon the other day."

His blue eyes search mine, and he swallows again. "Bennett is straight."

I grin. "You thought I was too."

He looks at me, confused and gnawing on his pink bottom lip. "Thought? Jesus, you're out now?"

I grin, bringing my hand up to cup the back of his sweaty neck. I don't care. "Sure."

"Grady," he warns, shaking his head but not pulling away, "I can't be an—"

I stop him, "An experiment. I know. I don't experiment, though, and you fucking know that about me. I jump in. Headfirst. I fucking explore."

He rolls his eyes at me. "Right. That's the same thing."

"No, it's not," I argue. "Exploring is knowing that I fucking want this." I tug him closer to me, using my hold on his neck. "And diving into it. It's an adventure, Ry."

"One that ends. An experience you can say you had."

He sounds bitter, and I don't like it. "No. If you'll remember, I was more than happy to go exploring both fucking times. You're the one who ran away like a little bitch."

He shoves me back, forcing me to release him. "Don't call me a bitch."

I quickly recover and close the gap between us. "Don't be

one." I thread my fingers through his damp hair. "I don't know where this is going or what it will lead to. That's fucking life. I had no idea what signing with the label would lead to either. Or agreeing to sing at the World Series, but I fucking did it. I went on the adventure."

He looks lost, and I fucking hate it. Pulling him closer to me, I drop the towel from around my neck to the floor and rest my other hand on his hip, relishing the cut, hard muscle there. "I'm sweaty."

"I don't fucking care." I grin. "I'm not a chick."

"Neither am I." His lip curls up in a challenge, and I smile, seeing a hint of my best friend there. Not lost in bitterness. Definitely in his head but relaxing with me ever so slightly.

"I. Know." I bring my lips to his, smashing them together in a heated, hungry kiss that, thank fuck, he returns. He doesn't fight me or push me away.

Instead, his hands move to my ass, and he pulls me flush against him, and I feel his cock against mine through my trunks and his shorts, eliciting a hearty moan from me.

I want this. I want all of this with him.

"Grady . . ." He's breathless as he speaks against my lips.

"Ry. I'm not going to hurt you." My heart actually aches, thinking about when he left. Thinking about last night when he pushed me away. I want to ask him not to hurt me either, but I don't know if he can promise that. I know Ry.

"Are you sure about this? I mean really sure?"

I smile against his lips, my hand roaming over his taut back, loving how the muscles ripple with each touch. *Who knew I was into muscles?* "Yes. I'm sure. I'm sure about you, Ry. The other shit we can figure out."

"Like me having a dick?"

I laugh but thrust my hips forward, sliding my erection against his and moaning at the sensation. "I don't think that's going to be a problem."

"What about everything else?" I'm sure he means our careers and that we're both in the public eye. And my dad being a fucking bigot and a preacher. And so on. But I don't care. I just use my hold on his hair to tug his head back and look into his eyes.

"There's nothing else. Just you and me. That's it, and that's all that fucking matters." His throat is pulled tight, and I lean down, licking the corded muscle of his neck and groaning from the salty taste of his skin. "You and me, Ry."

"Bell and Bailey." His voice is thick with lust, and I nod, nipping at his jaw before diving back into a heated kiss.

"Bailey and Bell."

His tongue sweeps over mine as he takes control, owning my mouth. I've never been more certain about anything in my life. My hands slide down his back, pulling him tighter against me as I dip down into his shorts and grasp his tight ass.

"You're driving me crazy," he gasps into my mouth but doesn't offer reprieve, kissing me again.

I smile into the kiss, wanting more. So much more, I push his shorts down without a second thought. I pull away from his lips as my forehead rests against his, and I look down, happy to see he wasn't wearing any underwear. His thick cock juts out and sticks straight up in greeting. "Oh, fuck."

"Regrets?"

"Hell, no." My hand moves to his long, hard shaft as I run my thumb over the glistening tip.

"Yes," he gasps as his hips buck forward, and I encircle his cock and kiss him again as he thrusts into my fist.

"Fuck, Grady." I love how breathless he is, how out of control as he looks between us and growls, "Show me."

My heart beats rapidly in my chest, my eyes not leaving his ripped abs as I release him momentarily and shove my trunks down.

"Fuck," he breathes and reaches out, taking me in his hand. "Fuck, Grady." His eyes lift to meet mine. "Is this really happening?"

I nod, not really sure what happens next but knowing I fucking want it. "Yes." I cup the back of his head and kiss his lips. "Yes." Kissing him deeper, I reach for his cock again, marveling in the difference.

I've only held my own cock before, but the feeling of his in my hand as I give him pleasure . . . That's fucking indescribable.

And I'm lost in his touch as he jerks me slowly while we kiss. I groan loudly and jut my hips forward angrily when he unexpectedly releases me. "No."

He merely smiles, bringing his hand up to his mouth and dragging his tongue over his hand, soaking it in spit before moving back to my dick. The slick feeling only adds to the euphoria as he whispers, "Nothing worse than a dry hand job."

I chuckle and then do the same, but before I know it, he's pushed my hand away, moving us so my back is against the wall and wrapping his hand around both of our solid lengths. "Holy. Fuck."

He grins as he kisses me, and we both thrust into his large hand. "I know. It would be better with lube."

"Next time." I look down between us, marveling at our cocks moving together. I'm slightly longer, but he has more girth. *Holy. Fuck.*

"Oh God, Ry." My balls draw up tight, and I know I'm close

to blowing my load. A tingling feeling runs down my spine, and all I feel is pleasure.

"Come with me, Grady."

That's all I need to hear before ropes of cum spurt between us, his hand and our cocks are covered, and it seems to be all he needs before he throws his head back with a hoarse cry, his release joining mine.

"Holy fucking shit." I look at him. "It's never felt like that. Never."

He grins. It's weary, but it's real. "Just wait."

I pull him in for another mind-bending kiss. "I can't fucking wait."

And I can't. Whatever this is, I'm all in.

RYAN

Oh. Fuck.

So much for being strong.

I know, without a doubt, I'm going to regret this, but I can't seem to bring myself to care. For so goddamn long, I've followed all the rules. The only times I've given in, I made damn sure to do it quietly, use NDAs, and never see them again.

But with Grady . . . that's not going to happen.

The stubborn fucker isn't going anywhere, and I'm glad.

"We're sticky," I say dumbly as my fingers trace the lines of his abs. They're hard and defined but not obsessively so. I love the feeling of his skin under my fingers.

His flesh against mine.

But I'm terrified to love it, to love this feeling and get lost in it.

I'm afraid to move. I don't want this to end. I'm worried he's going to look at me and say *"That was fun and all, but I'm definitely into chicks."*

Thankfully, Grady, being Grady, doesn't let me get too lost in my own toxic thoughts, and instead, his hands grip the sides of my face, and he forces me to look him in the eyes. "Then, we should shower."

I nod numbly as he kicks off his swim trunks, and I do the same with my shorts before he takes my hand and leads me to the master bath. He whistles when he sees the large bathroom with marble tile, a jacuzzi tub, and a shower big enough for five. Not that I've ever had anyone in here.

Showering with someone always seems too intimate to me, for some reason.

"Together?" I look at him, and he just shakes his head at me before walking to the shower, climbing in, and turning the water on.

"Get your ass in here, Bailey." he shouts, and I follow with a stupid fucking grin on my face. "He smiles," Grady says as I walk into the shower and close the glass door.

"Shut the fuck up."

He chuckles at that, letting the water run over his toned body. "Yeah, if I did that, I wouldn't be me, now, would I?"

"No. You wouldn't." I walk under the other showerhead and let the water spray over my face, not caring that my naked ass is on display. I think we're past that point.

I gasp, actually let a fucking gasp escape my mouth, when his strong arms wrap around me from behind. "I'm not going anywhere."

I close my eyes, letting the water run over my face as I try to chase away every insecurity threatening to come in and destroy this feeling. "Grady . . ." My voice sounds strangled and vulnerable, but I can't change it.

Not with him.

He turns me around, letting his hands rest on my shoulders. "I'm not going anywhere."

"How is this so easy for you?"

"Easy?"

I nod, looking into those fucking evergreen eyes that haunt me day and night. "Yeah. You decide to start fucking around with a guy, and that's just it? You flip a switch, and you're fucking hard for a guy?"

I'm being an asshole. I know that's not how this shit works, but he makes everything seem effortless. After my first time with a guy, I was paranoid as fuck for a year that he would tell his cousin about what happened. Or anyone. Hell, sometimes that fear creeps up out of nowhere even still.

Today at the coffee shop when he was shouting loudly, I was sweating, just knowing someone would pick up on the fact that we'd kissed the night before.

Rational?

Hell no.

Real?

Yeah.

I'm afraid all the fucking time. I say I don't care if I'm outed, that if it happens, it happens. But could I really handle it? Would I be okay? Seeing that disappointed look on my dad's face. Seeing my fans' disappointment that the man they worship just so happens to fuck men.

It shouldn't matter. I'm not ashamed of my sexuality, but bile sneaks up my throat thinking about facing it all.

It's crippling.

"Talk to me." Grady leans his forehead against mine in his signature move as water slides down my back.

I shake my head, but he doesn't relent. His hand moves over my heart that's thundering in my chest.

"I'm hard for one fucking guy. One."

"Grady." I look into his eyes, lifting my head. "I . . ."

"I know. You're scared."

"Why aren't you?"

He smiles, his lips brushing over mine. "Because of this." He kisses the corner of my mouth. "And this." He moves down my neck. "Definitely this." Then, his mouth presses a kiss over my heart where his hand was.

"How is this so easy for you? Really, Grady?"

"It's not easy. It's going to be a real pain in the ass. I know that. I'm not delusional." He lifts back up and looks at me with so much candor. "But I go after what I want."

He wants me.

I can see it.

But for how long?

I can't bring myself to ask the question. I'm not ready for the answer. Not yet. I kiss his lips, grabbing the back of his neck and holding him there.

Right now—for once—I'm just going to live in the moment.

GRADY

"BE HONEST WITH ME." I turn my head and look at Ry. He's laying flat on his back on his bed, and I'm right next to him.

After our shower, we dried off but didn't bother putting on any clothes before lying down.

"I'm always honest with you." I brush my thumb over his cheek, taking him in. His jaw is as carved as the rest of him, but he has several days growth covering it now. His eyes are bright blue at the moment, although they definitely change with his mood, and his lips are puffy and pink. They might be my favorite thing.

"Grady. I'm serious. Are you really not freaking out right now?"

I sigh and drop my hand to my side, rolling to look up at the ceiling. "Fine. You know all the shit my father used to preach and how we would always laugh at him?"

He cringes, and rolls to his side when my head lolls to the side to look at him. "All that 'God hates gays' shit?"

I nod, my jaw clenching tight. "I never believed it. Not for a second. But . . ."

He eyes me cautiously, tucking his hand under his head and

propping up on his elbow. I'm fascinated by the muscles of his bicep pulling tight and drag my finger over his skin absently. "But what?"

"I tried my best to piss him off. Always. Smoking. Drinking. Staying out late. Skipping church."

"I remember." His lips pull up in a sexy smile.

"Yeah." I notice a tattoo on his right pec and let my fingers trail over the colorful art. "But I think in the back of my mind, I always knew . . ." I swallow tightly, not really proud of myself. "Kissing a guy would be the final straw with him."

He winces, and I flatten my hand over his heart. "So, when we kissed . . .?" He waits for me to fill in the blank.

"I wanted it. One hundred percent, Ry. But . . ." I sigh and roll to my side to face him., "Maybe the next day . . ." I shake my head. "Maybe I would have freaked out too. Knowing it would really set my father off."

He doesn't look as pissed-off at my admission as I thought he'd be. Instead, his large hand moves to my face, and a look of understanding crosses his. "I was afraid of that. I remember the shit he'd say in church and when his congregation wasn't around. I know what was pounded into your head day after day. Hell, my own parents thought the same shit."

I cover his hand with mine, looking him straight in the eye. "I never, ever believed it."

He smiles and nods slowly. "I know. I know your heart isn't ugly, Grady, but I thought you'd freak out."

"I may have, but I wouldn't have hurt you, Ry." My eyes drop to his full lips and then return to focus on his eyes. "Not on purpose."

"But now?"

"Now, what?" I whisper against his mouth because I'm really done fucking talking.

His hand moves to my chest, and he holds me at bay. "Now, are you freaking out?"

"Hell, no. I don't give a flying fuck what my father thinks. Not at all. I want nothing to do with him or any of the hate his so called 'church' spews."

I brush my lips over his while his hand is still between us. "What about your career? My career?"

"That could be tricky," I admit.

"What is this?" His voice is shaky.

"Always need a definition, huh, Ry?"

He nods, and I can't stop staring at him. I'd be lying if I hadn't noticed him before, but now that I've been this close to him and kissed him freely—I can't stop staring. I don't want to. "If there's no definition, someone will get hurt."

He's afraid. Ryan Bailey is one tough motherfucker, but I can tell just how scared he is right now. Afraid I'll hurt him.

"Okay." I think it over and nip on his earlobe, pulling a deep growl from him, the sound going straight to my balls and making my already aching dick harder.

Jesus, it's only been an hour since I last came, and I'm dying for another release.

My hand slides over his bare, firm ass, and I squeeze, pulling him closer to me. "No more fucking baristas." My voice is husky and full of rocks, but I don't care. I want to make this clear.

He groans and rolls his eyes. "I didn't *fuck* the barista, asshole."

"Well, no more anyone . . ." I nip his jaw, and he growls,

rolling us over so his body is on top of mine. I like the weight of him pressing down on me. "Only me."

His eyes search mine, and he gives a slight nod. "Only me."

I grin. "I suppose."

"Asshole." He leans down, his tongue finding my nipple and making it hard as he flicks over it, and then the fucker bites it.

"Ow, you're the asshole." He chuckles, but then pops it into his mouth, sucking hard and making my hips thrust forward with need. Our cocks slide together, both leaking from the tip and supplying enough slickness for us to grind against each other.

"Fuck," I gasp and pull his face down to mine, biting and sucking on his lower lip. "Fuck fuck fuck."

"Don't come yet."

"I'm no fucking chump."

He chuckles again, his body sliding down as his tongue trails over my stomach, the tattoo on my hip, and then my inner thigh. Everywhere but where I desperately need him. "We have three weeks to explore. I'm going to go over every fucking inch of you."

Holy shit. His mouth moves to my balls, sucking each one into his mouth, making me groan loudly, "Fuck, Ry. Don't tease me."

He releases my balls and grins up at me with a sureness I haven't seen in him for a long time. "I've got you." He moves to the head of my cock, covering it with his mouth and sucking it, his tongue moving over the tip.

"Fuck."

I can feel the fucker smiling around my cock before he takes it deeper in his mouth. Opening his throat, he takes me deep like a fucking champ, bobbing up and down, making me lose my mind.

"Yes. Fuck, I'm close." He pops off my dick, and I groan, looking down at him. "Don't fucking stop."

"How much do you trust me?"

"What?" I lean up on my elbows as he remains between my parted thighs. "So much. All the fucking trust. Why?"

He grins, slipping his finger into his mouth and wetting it, his spit sliding down the digit. "Because I'm going to make it really, really fucking good for you."

His mouth takes my cock back deep into his throat before I feel the pad of his slick finger on my asshole. I clench tight, not sure I'm ready for that, but he doesn't push in. He just teases as his mouth drives me fucking wild, and I relax slightly.

"Ry," I moan softly, my fingers threading through his hair.

My hips start moving with his mouth as I come closer and closer to ecstasy. I watch him grind against the mattress, sucking me off while slowly pressing his finger inside my ass. It doesn't hurt, maybe a little burn, but my focus is on his mouth as he tries to suck me dry.

When his finger is fully inside, he crooks it at an angle, hitting something inside me just fucking right, making my hips piston forward into his throat. He gags slightly, the rumble making my balls draw up tight. "Holy fucking shit. Do that again."

I can feel him smiling, and he does it again. Pleasure zaps through me, up my spine and making my fucking toes curl.

"Oh, fuck. I'm going to come, Ry."

He only sucks harder as he ruts against the mattress.

"Fuuuuck." I come hard, releasing into his mouth, and I feel him swallowing around my cock and sending me even further over the edge.

When I catch my breath, he moves up my body, his mouth crashing to mine. I moan into the kiss, tasting my salty release and not giving a fuck. It's with him.

"Jesus fucking Christ. That's what I've been missing? All this time?"

He smiles, and I look down when I feel something wet on my thigh. His dick is spent, and I realize he came while sucking me off.

"Holy fuck, that's hot." I kiss him harder and tuck his body beneath mine.

I can't believe I've wasted so much time not doing this.

RYAN

"Now what?" I lift my head to look at Grady, who has one arm tucked behind his head in all his confident, cocky glory. My head is still resting on his chest, and I'm a sticky fucking mess, but I'm too satiated to move.

I can't believe this is real, but there's no denying that he wants this. At least his body does. And I'm a selfish, greedy bastard because I meant what I said—I'm going to enjoy every second of the next three weeks, even if what comes after will kill me.

"Now, we order food because I'm fucking starving."

"You mean you haven't become a domestic goddess in the past seven years?"

I shake my head at him but am unable to hold back my full smile. "Nope. You?"

An easy grin is plastered on his face, and I take a moment to bask in the glow of his happiness. "Fuck, no. Ordering sounds good to me."

There are so many doubts running through my head, but I'm determined not to let them come out. We clean up, get dressed in sweats, and then order pizza. When it arrives, we go back to my bed and feast.

"So, your parents really pretend you aren't gay?"

I lean back against my headboard, finishing a bigass bite of pizza. "Do we really have to talk about it?"

"Yeah." He scoots closer to me. "Yeah, we do. I've missed a lot these past seven years, and I want to know it all, Ry."

I turn to look him in the eyes, and I'm amazed at how he does that. No one can make me open up like Grady. No one. I'm so used to keeping this shit tucked away, but he's here for a couple of days, and I'm willing to open up about everything. "Are you really that surprised? They were in the front pew of your father's church every fucking Sunday since before you and I were born."

He bristles, and I know his father is a sore subject, but so are my parents. "That's still fucked up."

"At least they don't hate me. Or they don't act like they do. They call once a week. They just avoid . . ."

"Part of you."

"Goddamn it, Grady." I sit up straighter, ready to bail, but manage to keep my ass on the bed. "I don't want to think about this."

"How long have you avoided thinking or talking about it? How much of yourself have you had to hide to keep other people happy?" His eyes bore into mine. "How much have you given up?"

"You're one to talk."

"Hey, I . . ." He must rethink what he was about to say because he pauses and then takes a deep breath. "I didn't know I liked dick until recently. So it's not something I had to hide."

I smile inwardly, but then my smile actually makes it to my

face. Because he could still deny what we did. Call it a fluke or say he wasn't sure about what's going on. But no, not Grady. He said he likes dick, and I can't stop the goofy-ass grin from forming when I've had a perpetual straight face for so many years. "You've had to hide plenty. I mean hell, aren't you currently in a fake relationship?"

He grabs his phone from the table next to my bed and checks it. "Yup. Still in a fake relationship as of now. I really need to call Vicky sometime."

Even knowing it's fake, I don't know the circumstances, and it's another punch to the heart. "See?"

His hand runs through his thick black hair that I now know is really fucking soft. "Okay, so I've had to hide some shit from the world, but not that. It's bullshit that you can't be who you are, Ry. Because who you are is really fucking great."

I lean back against the headboard, settling in. "So are you. It's the price we pay for fame. One I knew I'd have to deal with even before I accepted my scholarship."

He finishes his pizza and then takes a drink of water before turning to me on the bed and cupping my face in his hands, but he doesn't kiss me. He just gazes into my eyes and fractures my heart into more pieces. "It's never been like this. Never."

"What hasn't?"

I don't know if I can take the answer. "I've been with so many women. Probably too many. But it was never like this. Ever. I never got lost in just a fucking kiss. And the other stuff? It was never like that either."

It's too heavy. My heart actually fucking aches with hope threatening to etch it's way inside, and I can't take it. Instead, I take a play from Grady. "And I haven't even fucked you yet."

He cocks his head to the side, releasing me, and for a minute

I think he's going to call me on my shit, but he doesn't. He's Grady. "Hmm, have I said I'm going to let you fuck me?"

I laugh and lay my head against his chest, settling into the crook of his arm. "No. But you're definitely going to fuck me." I look up at him, seeing his throat is pulled tight with an emotion I'm betting is excitement. "If you want to."

He nods his head comically fast. "I want that. I want to." He swallows hard, his Adam's Apple bobbing in his throat.

I grin. "Soon."

"Soon," he agrees, and I can see the nerves mixed with his excitement.

Holy shit, I managed to frazzle Grady fucking Bell.

RYAN

WAKING up next to Grady is something I could easily get used to. Which is fucking terrifying. Before I get too lost in watching his sleeping form sprawled out next to me, my phone rings, and I groan when I see it's Jenny.

"Fuck me."

"I'm up for it."

I roll my eyes and chuckle when I'm met with a grin from my best friend and then grab my phone, answering it. "Hey, Jenny."

"Oh, you're alive. Good to know."

I stretch, ignoring her tone because that's just Jenny. "Yeah, lucky you. What's up?"

"My. Cock." Grady's voice is quiet, but I still give him a shake of my head as he starts to trail kisses down my bare torso. Still, I don't tell him to stop.

I'm not fucking stupid.

"You have the parade. In two fucking hours. You need to get your ass here."

"Fuck." Grady looks up at me with a curious look.

"The parade," I say to Grady, but it's Jenny who speaks next, probably thinking I'm talking to her.

"Yes. The parade. A victory parade in your honor."

"And the team's."

Grady's lips trail over my stomach and then back up, leaving kisses over the short beard I have going now.

"Yeah, whatever. I don't get paid for any of them. So, as far as I'm concerned, it's your victory."

I nod absently as Grady starts to suck on my neck, and I can't find any fucks to give about anything Jenny is saying. "I'll be there."

"You need to be early, Ryan. I mean it. Get your ass up and go."

"Fine." I hang up, placing my phone next to me and gripping the back of Grady's hair, pulling his mouth to mine for a hungry good-morning kiss.

"Good morning." He grins but doesn't pull away, and my hand is still in his hair. "Parade is today?"

I nod, not wanting to go. "I'd rather stay here with you."

"Nope." He kisses my lips again and then jumps off the bed. "We're going to that fucking parade. You earned it. You worked your ass off for it."

I notice the hard-on he's sporting in his sweats and stand up, slipping my hand under the waistband and grabbing his long cock. "I'd rather play."

"Fuck, Ry," he whispers as I start to stroke his length. But then his hand captures my wrist. "Parade. When does it start?"

"Two hours. We have time."

He swallows, his eyes lowering to where I'm still grasping his erection. "No. Coffee. Parade. Then back here."

I reluctantly release him because I can see I'm not going to win this argument even if he's tempted. "Coffee?"

"Yeah, I know a place." I roll my eyes, but he slaps my ass. "Come on. Shower. Then coffee."

Thankfully, he agrees to a mutual jerk off session in the shower because who the fuck doesn't have time for that? Seeing him watching me as I stroked my dick until I came was one of the hottest things in my life, but I know there's a hell of a lot more to come.

When we get to the coffee shop, we're greeted by Justin and his bubbly personality, but Grady cuts in front of me this time. "Well, good morning, Justin."

Oh. Fuck. "Good morning, Mr. Bell. Black coffee for you today?"

Justin is just as sunny as always, but I see a flicker of something ornery in Grady's eyes. "No." He looks over at me and then back to Justin with a shit-eating grin on his handsome face. "You know, I've really been into trying new things lately, Justin. What would you recommend?"

Justin seems to take this as a barista challenge, but I know what Grady is really talking about, and it isn't coffee. "Well, let me think." Justin puts his finger on his chin. "Since you're used to plain coffee, I wouldn't get too crazy right away."

Grady eyes me with hunger, making my dick stir in my jeans—the motherfucker—and then moves his attention back to Justin. "I don't mind getting crazy, exploring my options."

His voice has a low sultry tone. I look at Justin, who's noticeably flushed but uncertain. "Um . . . sure." His voice cracks, and I'm two seconds away from ripping Grady out of here. What the fuck is he doing? "In that case, I recommend the latte macchiato. It's my specialty." He smiles at me. "I've been trying to get this guy to try it for a while now, but the calories scared him away."

Grady's eyes drag over my arms and torso in a lazy, way too dangerous way before he turns his attention back to Justin. "Yeah, I guess you don't get that body with those kind of drinks."

"Jesus Christ," I say it low enough, but Grady hears me.

"Um." Justin is clearly flustered now. "Right."

"I'll take my usual, Justin. Thank you."

He busies himself with our order, and I turn to Grady, my jaw clenched. "What the hell are you doing?"

He shrugs. "Just having a little fun."

Bullshit.

We grab our coffees, and I pay, walking outside with Grady toward my truck before I dig into what the fuck that was. "Seriously? Fun. He's a nice guy. What are you trying to do?"

"Nice?" Grady's eyes meet mine, and I see fire in them. Not fun. Just fucking fire. It's hot, I'm not going to lie.

"Yeah. Nice."

"He wants to fuck you. Or you to fuck him. Whatever. And it's bullshit . . ." he says, standing too fucking close so he can look me right in the eye, and it's intense, too intense for being out in public, "that I can't just pull you into my arms and let that fucker know that you're mine."

"Yours?" I nearly choke the word out.

"Mine." His voice is a deep growl that shoots straight to my already interested dick.

But before I can respond, a car pulls up, and I instinctively back up and turn away before the photographer jumps out.

Fuck. That was too close.

"Hey, Ryan. You guys on your way to the parade?"

"You know it!" Grady shouts out, holding up his cup of coffee, winking at the camera before climbing into the truck.

I'm too flustered and way too hard to answer as I retreat behind the wheel and start the truck, closing the door.

"You better wave to the camera or they're going to peg you as an asshole."

"Goddamn it." I know he's right and make sure to plaster a fake smile on my face, giving a wave before pulling out of my parking spot.

Fucking Grady. He's going to out me less than an hour after waking up in bed with me for the first time.

GRADY

YESTERDAY WAS awesome watching Ry and his teammates celebrate their victory with the entire metro area. The place was packed full and a sea of blue.

Last night was even better, sharing his bed and exploring each other's bodies. We haven't gone too far yet, but I'm fucking ready.

More than ready.

No part of me cares that his body is male and not female like I'm used to. His hard edges and muscular lines turn me the fuck on, along with the fact that it's Ry—my best friend.

"Morning." God, I even love his fucking voice. It's deep and low, rumbling in my ear.

"Good morning." I open my eyes and see him peering down at me like he can't believe I'm here. "Are you ready for a repeat of last night?" I waggle my eyebrows and move my body so it's resting on top of his.

He smiles, his hand sliding over my cheek. "Yeah. I'm definitely ready for more of that."

Just as our mouths start to drift toward each other, there's a loud bang downstairs followed by a shrill voice that makes my dick instantly deflate. "Ryan, get your ass down here."

"Why the fuck does your agent have a key?"

He groans, resting his hands over his eyes. "Fuck. She pretty much controls my life. It seemed like a good idea at the time."

I shake my head, my body still on top of his. "It's not."

He lays a quick kiss on my lips before sliding out from under me where he fucking belongs and tugs on a pair of sweats, sweeping his hand through his messy bedhead. "If I don't go out there, she's going to come in here."

I reluctantly climb out of bed and grab a pair of sweats myself, pulling them on as I grumble. He laughs as he watches me and then grabs a baseball cap, tugging it on over his head.

I couldn't give a fuck and follow him to the foyer to face his ballbusting agent. "There you are." She looks behind Ryan and sees me. "And of course, he's in tow." I resist the urge to flip her off, but she's actually smiling. "There are pictures of you two everywhere."

We all walk into Ry's living room and take our seats—Jenny in a chair on her own and Ry and me on the couch. "Okay? Why are you smiling?" Ryan asks the question I was silently wondering.

Her dark eyebrows pull together like we're both stupid. "Because there are pictures of you two all over the place. People are eating this bromance up."

Bromance. Pretty sure my eyes just darted out of my head, but Ry just leans back against the couch. "So bromances are a good thing? Me taking a picture with a fan, not so good?"

She rolls her eyes at him, crossing her thin little arms. "You're still pissy about that? Come on, Ryan. You know the game by now."

I'm pretty sure he's sick to death of said game, but I manage to keep my mouth shut.

"Yeah, yeah," he grumbles, back to being a grumpy motherfucker.

"Anyway." She waves her hand in our direction. "Keep this shit up, okay? It's good. It's very good. Fans are eating it up."

Yeah, she's happy now, but that's because she has no idea where my tongue was just last night.

Ry must sense my thoughts because he shoots me a warning look, and I can't wait to get this bitch out of here so I can help him relax.

"I booked a show for you two tomorrow."

That gets my attention. "A show?"

She nods. "Yeah. You guys are going on *The Tonight Show* via video. It's all set up. You'll just answer questions about your childhood and how you reconnected. They'll love it."

Ry looks pale, but I'm pissed. "What the fuck? You aren't my agent."

She rolls her eyes at me, and it's not cute when she does it like when Ry does it. "Oh, please. As if I didn't contact Waylon. He's completely on board with this."

My mouth pops open in shock, and she again rolls her eyes.

She turns her attention solely to Ry. "Every appearance ups your popularity. Which, in turn, makes your price tag higher."

"You're fucking lovely."

"Eat me." She glares at me.

"Not a fucking chance, princess."

She's shooting daggers at me, but Ryan intervenes, sitting forward. "Guys, get along." He eyes his agent. "We'll do it."

She stands up, her heels clicking on the wooden floor as she walks over, zoning in on me. "Thank fuck you aren't my problem, but you do increase his price. So, thank you." She purses her lips, kissing at me condescendingly, and I keep my ass planted on the couch.

She tells Ry she'll be in touch before walking out the door, and I turn to him, curious about why the hell he would agree to this. "You really want to do an interview together? Perpetuating this whole 'bromance' bullshit?"

"We're friends."

"Who are fucking," I deadpan.

His expression switches from concern, straight to fucking lust as he moves his body closer to mine. "Not quite fucking. Not yet."

"Don't try and distract me, asshole."

He grins, and damn if it doesn't work because him smiling is every fucking thing. "What if people pick up on it?"

"I've done several interviews. So far, so good."

"But with me right next to you?" My hand grazes his thigh, and he shudders, so fucking responsive to my touch.

"Well, you can't be doing *that* shit."

He straddles my legs, his weight heavy but nice as his hands come up and grasp my hair at the sides. "Ry . . ."

"What?" he asks, but I'm lost in the sensation of his growing erection grinding against my own.

"We should shower." My hands clutch his ass. "Eat." He grins and nods, resting his forehead against mine. "Maybe eventually talk."

His grip tightens in my hair, and I sense his nerves. "Talk about what?"

I increase my hold on his ass, massaging the firm cheeks in my hand. "Everything."

Now he looks worried, and I can't imagine why. I mean, his

ass is literally in my hands at the moment. It's not like I'm going anywhere or want to. "Everything?" He swallows tightly, and I watch the motion, bringing one hand up to drag a finger over his throat.

"Yeah. The future. Our careers. All that shit."

He's gone back to my grumpy Ry, climbing off my lap and nodding. "Okay. I guess we should go shower."

He doesn't ask me to join him in his room, and I sit there, unsure about what the fuck just happened. *He doesn't want to talk about the future?*

Am I reading everything wrong?

RYAN

I'M FUCKING CRIPPLED by his words earlier. Talk about everything. Everything—as in, *Hey this was fun and all, but I think I'm going back to chicks?*

Fuck.

We've avoided each other most of the day, which was fairly easy with it being a big house. Grady spent most of the day out by the pool while I spent mine in the gym, trying to work out my frustration.

It's not working.

I know I need to face him and just get it over with. I find him downstairs in the music room, the sound of the guitar leading me there.

I freeze in the doorway, knowing the song instantly. It's a newer one, released a few months ago.

The words send a tremor through me, leaving me motionless as I listen to the acoustic live version in my basement.

Are you out there?

Are you free?

Or are you trapped like me?

Can you go about living your life?
Or are you like I am?
Stuck in this hellish wonderland . . .

The lyrics repeat again, but then he looks up and sees me, his fingers and voice halting. "Hey."

"Hi," I say dumbly, still boneless and unmoving. When I heard the song for the first time I was stunned stupid. I listened to it one more time and then never again. I couldn't face it. I couldn't let myself hope that it meant so much more than just a hit song.

That he wrote it about me.

Finally, I find my voice again. "Are you ready for that talk yet?"

He puts the guitar down and nods as I approach him on the couch he's sitting on. "Why the hell are you freaking out about talking?" He looks hurt, and I hate that I avoided him all day.

"Look, just say it. Okay?" I sit next to him. "Say that this was fun, but you don't want it to go any further."

"What?" His brow wrinkles in confusion. "That's what you thought I meant by talking about everything?"

"What else could it be?"

"Our careers. How the fuck we can do this when we both travel a shitload. How we can make it work."

It. Work.

As in a relationship. I'm fucking frozen yet again. "It?"

He sighs, frustrated with me and maybe a little hurt? "It. Us. Whatever the fuck you want to call it."

Holy shit, there's an us.

"You want there to be an us?"

He turns to look straight at me and then places his hand on

the side of my face, preventing me from looking away. "There was always an us."

Holy. Shit. "Grady . . ."

"What? You don't want that? If not, tell me now."

"Of course, I do. But you're . . ." He moves his hand over my mouth and shakes his head firmly.

"We're way past me being straight, considering your tongue was in my ass last night, and I fucking loved it."

I gulp. Actually gulp. Shocked and turned the fuck on. Elated by his words. He removes his hand from my mouth, and I nod. "Okay."

"Okay. This isn't a phase. I have no idea what sexuality I am. and I don't fucking care. I'm in this. I like what we've done, and I want more. But we can't deny it'll have an impact on our careers."

"You sound more like me than you right now."

He grins, leaning back into the couch and relaxing. "Look, you know me. I jump into everything, usually without a thought, but things that matter . . ." His eyes meet mine with so much sincerity in them, I nearly choke on the emotion. "There has only ever been music and you . . . So, those things . . . I put effort into them. I make them work. And I want this to work."

"I do too, Grady." God, I want that more than anything, but I'm terrified to admit just how much.

If this crashes and burns, I'm pretty sure I'm done.

"Good. Now, you have a contract negotiation coming up, right?"

I nod. "Yeah. I've been ordered to be good."

He gives me a wicked smile and moves closer. "Oh, you've been very, very good."

I chuckle at that and start to relax. "Jenny will freak the fuck out if we out me."

"We won't. We're capable of keeping this a secret. The bromance that everyone thinks they want, we can do that. We've been friends forever."

I stand up, reaching out for his hand. "Let's go discuss this in my room."

He doesn't argue, just hops up as we head upstairs. When we're in my bed with our shoes and socks off, he's the one to start the discussion again. "I've watched you play the game. You may be tired as fuck of all the PR bullshit, but you still love playing baseball."

I nod, swallowing thickly and knowing he's right. "I do. I really do."

He cups my face in his large hand, his fingers calloused from years of playing the guitar. "Then you can't let anything else get in the way."

"I would for you." And it's true. Completely, 100 percent true. I would give up everything to be with him.

"I won't let you." His lips graze mine. "We can be discreet. We can figure it out."

"You love the music too. Your career is important. I've watched you when you play. I've watched you work the crowd. No matter how large or small. You love it."

He smiles, and it's all confidence. "You've been to my concerts?"

I nod, not bothering to lie. "A few over the years. And you fucking love it."

He looks like he wants to say something, but quickly changes his mind. "I do. But I want this with you."

"What would your label say if you started fucking a guy?"

He bristles, and I know he hates that part of fame as much as I do. "I doubt they would be okay with it. They pretend to care about all people, but it's not the truth. My brand is the bad boy who some woman can someday change."

I nod, already knowing that. "Yeah. I think that's really what the baseball world wants to believe about me."

"I know it is." He faces me while we lay on my bed and holds me there. "Okay. No more talking. We do it the Grady Bell way."

I laugh, "And what way is that?"

"We go for it. We do exactly what we want, jumping in headfirst, and we don't fucking worry. It'll work out. We'll be careful in public."

"It's all going to blow up."

"Maybe. But for right now, I just want this." He leans forward and kisses me deeply, pulling a deep groan from me. I've missed him all day, and he was right here.

"I do too. Just one more question," I say against his lips, and he smiles.

"What?"

"Did you write "Hellish Wonderland" about me?"

He grins smugly. "What do you think?"

I bite his bottom lip and then suck on it before meeting his eyes. "I think I want you to fuck me."

Now it's his turn to gulp loudly as he nods. "I'd like that."

"Good." I kiss him again, letting my body drift over his.

I decide taking the Grady Bell route sounds really fucking good right now.

GRADY

HOLY FUCK, I'm nervous. I've never been this nervous in my life. We undress, kissing and taking our time, which I'm fucking grateful for, considering the nerves firing in the pit of my stomach. He's done this before. He's been with other men and knows what he's doing.

Me? I've only been with women.

What if I fuck it all up? What if I hurt him? Or I'm just plain lame?

"Hey." His lips brush over mine. "Breathe."

"I'm breathing."

He cocks an eyebrow, and it's hard to think with his hard body pressed against mine. "Are you sure about that?"

"Shut the fuck up." He grins and reaches next to him, opening a drawer and depositing a bottle of lube and a condom onto the bed next to us.

"Talk to me."

"I've never done anal." He quirks a brow, and I think, for the first time in my life, I'm fucking blushing.

"Never?"

I shake my head. "No. And I don't want to fucking hurt you. Although you're making it a little easier now."

He grins, full of confidence and kisses my lips, spreading assurance through me. "It's okay, rockstar. I've been down this road a couple of times before, and although it's been a while, I'm fucking ready for you." He kisses me again, his lips trailing down my neck, and I close my eyes, trying to gain control of my thundering heart and shaky hands.

"How do we do it?" He laughs, and I growl, "I know how to fucking do it, I just mean like face-to-face or do you roll over?" Christ. I sound like a fucking virgin.

I guess, in this sense, I am. He shakes his head at me, lying flat on his back. "Prep and lube. And then, however you want me."

I settle my naked body on his, relishing the feeling of his warm skin wrapping the hard muscle underneath. When I look down into his eyes, so fucking blue and full of lust and want, I shudder.

The things he fucking does to me.

His big hand slides over my heart, and his smile is kind. "You're trembling for me."

I nod and lean down to kiss him. "I only remember shaking from nerves one time before. Right before my first live show. It was nerves, but it was also just plain excitement because I knew it was the start of something great, but this . . ." I kiss him again softly. "This is even better. This is everything."

"Jesus," he breathes, grasping the back of my hair and pulling me to his mouth as he kisses me deeply. His other hand reaches for something, and then I hear a lid popping before his hand moves between us.

I release his mouth to look down where he's using one

finger to move in and out of his hole, preparing himself for me. "Holy fuck, that's hot."

"Join me?" He holds out the bottle of lube, and I take it, knowing I want to take my time with him. I sit up on my knees, grabbing the condom, opening the foil packet and then sliding it down over my cock before lubing it and my fingers up generously.

I watch him fuck himself with his fingers before I grab his wrist and remove his hand, easily sliding my finger inside his tight heat.

"You're so fucking tight, Ry. I can't wait to be inside you."

He throws his head back in the pillows, moving his hips along with my finger. "Another."

I oblige, adding another finger and stretching him, my cock screaming to be where my fingers are. But I wasn't kidding—I don't want to hurt him. I want to ruin him for all other men. I want him to think about me and me only.

I crook my finger, seeking out that magical spot he's found in me many times, and when I hit it, his hips jolt off the bed, and he groans loudly, "Fuck. Yes. Do that again, Grady."

I do, but only once because I don't want him coming yet, not until I'm buried inside him. "Are you ready for me, Bailey?"

"Jesus. Fuck." His hips buck with my fingers as he says, "Yes. Yes. Fuck me."

I remove my fingers and move back up over his body, the nerves once again kicking in. "I want this more than I've ever wanted anything in my life."

He grabs the back of my neck with one hand and my ass with the other, urging me forward. "Then fucking take it."

I move my cock to his entrance, prodding gently at first, making him growl again and kiss me with frustration and fury.

"You aren't going to hurt me. But if you do, I'll fucking love it."

"You're bossy in bed."

"Damn straight." He smiles, biting my bottom lip. "Fuck me like you mean it."

I can't take it anymore. Sliding the head of my cock past the first ring of muscle, I swear stars flash behind my eyes. I'm not even sure whose voice it is that makes a strangled unholy moan, but I think it might be both of us.

"Yes."

"God, you feel fucking amazing." I inch forward, my forehead resting against his as I push inside. "Fuck, Ry. You're the tightest fucking thing I've ever been inside."

I can't even make out his words as he lifts his legs up, allowing me to sink all the way inside him and even deeper.

"Holy fuck."

He grins. "Fuck me, Bell. Don't hold back."

And I don't. I thrust inside his tight hole over and over again, savoring every time his ass clenches around me, strangling my cock. "Please tell me you're close."

"Touch me."

I grab the lube and spread it over his cock that's already leaking at the tip and jerk him in tandem with each thrust into his ass. "Fuck."

"Yeah, fuck." I shift my hips, hitting him deep and making him curse. "Holy shit. Yes. Right fucking there, Grady."

His voice, the strangled cries are sending me over the edge and fast. "Come, Ry. I can't hold on much longer."

"I'm right fucking there. Don't hold back."

I pound into him over and over again, not wanting the moment to end but needing to come more than I need to breathe. "Oh, God. I'm gonna come." When I feel a hot burst of cum over my hand, I finally let myself go, losing my mind when I hear him moan, "Yes, Grady. Come in my ass." I fucking lose it, coming hard into the condom, hating that there's a barrier between us.

"Holy fuck." We're a sweaty sticky mess, but I'm not moving off him. My lips meet his as we kiss, and my fingers slide through his hair. "Do you really want that?"

"Want what?" he asks breathlessly.

"Me to come inside of you?" His ass clenches around my softening cock, and damn if my body doesn't want to fucking rally.

"Yeah, I fucking want that. When was the last time you were tested?"

I think about it. "It's been a few months."

"Me too. I always use condoms, but just in case, we should go get tested. I know a discreet place."

I nod in agreement. "I've always used condoms too." I lean down and kiss him. "I can't fucking wait to be inside you bare."

"You did alright for your first time, rockstar."

I roll my eyes, and then he rolls our bodies over so he's on top of me. "Please, I blew your fucking mind."

He laughs easily at that, leaving a peck on my mouth. "You did. You really fucking did. But how is it that you haven't ever done anal?"

I shrug, feeling slightly insecure, but this is Ry. "Every single hookup has been a blur. Only about the easiest, fastest way to get off. I haven't put in the work for any kind of trust and barely even remember names."

Again, my cheeks are blazing red, but he doesn't look disgusted. "I get that. Believe me. It's why I haven't bottomed for a long, long time. I haven't wanted to put in the work to get to the trust part."

Pride and happiness shoots through me because even though we've both hooked up with people before, this is the first time we've felt a true connection.

And I wouldn't want it to be with anyone other than my Bailey.

"Do we really have to do this?" I laugh at Grady's whining about *The Tonight Show* appearance, but I don't blame him. Even though my ass is still sore from last night, I want nothing more than to drag him back to bed.

"Yes. It'll help." I grab his hips and pull him to me. "You raise my price tag, remember?"

He laughs at that, easy and calm. His grin is something I can get lost in. "Well, I suppose this goes to our retirement plan then?"

I swallow, looking into his eyes, trying to see if he's fucking with me. But I only see honesty. "Retirement?"

"Yeah." His lips brush over mine. "When I'm a washed-up rockstar and your body has had enough of playing . . . We'll travel. Maybe move to an island."

I grin. "You can't swim." The fucker sinks like a rock in water.

"Guess it will be an island we never leave."

I laugh but release his hips when I hear Jenny's voice coming from the living room. We're still in my room after a shower we shared, but we're both dressed and ready now.

"Fuck, Medusa is here." I shake my head at yet another nickname Grady has for her.

"Not original."

He flips me off, and we walk into my living room where a camera crew has a setup going for the live interview, and Jenny and Waylon are busy directing them. "Fucking finally." Jenny is her usual self as she walks over to us in a sleek, black designer skirt and crisp white shirt.

"Sorry. Had to make ourselves pretty," I say, and Grady is right by my side.

"They're ready for you two. Don't fuck this up."

"We'd never mess with your paycheck, Jen-nay." I turn to Grady, shaking my head at his Forrest Gump impression, but I can't help smiling.

She flips him off and walks back over to the camera crew, obsessive over every single angle.

"She really hates you."

Grady shrugs his large shoulders, tossing me a wicked grin. "But you don't."

"No. No, I don't."

His smile only widens. "In fact, you kind of fucking love me."

I can't argue with it, but I'm not sure what sense he means when he uses the word "love." Like a friend? Or so much fucking more? Because my mind and heart are starting to lean toward the latter. Or maybe they were already there, and it's too much for right now.

"Okay, you two are going to have to get this under control." I startle at the sound of Waylon's voice behind us. He's quiet, but when he stands between us and eyes us both, a cold, worried shiver slides through me.

"Get what under control?" Grady asks, looking behind us at Jenny, who thankfully is preoccupied.

"This . . ." He keeps his voice low as he waves between Grady and me. "The obvious flirting."

"We aren't flirting," I object quickly. Maybe too quickly because Waylon pins me with a knowing look.

"You are. You're both standing here like you want to devour the fuck out of each other. Like you've definitely seen the other one's face when they come."

Grady nudges him. "Hey, shut it."

Waylon isn't bothered by the nervous edge in Grady's tone and shrugs. "It's hot. I'm not going to lie, and some people may think it's just this bromance bullshit Jenny is trying to sell. But I'm telling you . . . some people will definitely pick up on it."

Shit. Shit. Shit. I look at Grady. "Did you tell him?"

Grady looks slightly guilty. "Not exactly."

"Look, trust me." Waylon steals my attention. "Your secret is totally safe with me, but you guys have to tone down the bedroom eyes."

"They aren't bedroom eyes," Grady tries to argue.

"Bullshit." He turns to Grady. "Having said all that, though, I so want details later." He winks at me as he walks away, and I stare at Grady wide-eyed and freaked the fuck out.

"I didn't tell him about last night." His eyes plead with me to listen, but he doesn't touch me or move closer. "I promise. And I'm not going to."

"It's fine. You guys are friends." I feel numb and I fucking hate it. I was on a high earlier today, but maybe Waylon is right. How the hell are we going to hide the fact that we're fucking?

"Ry, listen to me." I look into his eyes. "It's going to be fine. I promise. Everyone is just going to see what we want them to."

"This was a stupid idea."

"An idea pushed by your agent." He has to point it out, but Jenny doesn't have the facts, unlike Waylon apparently.

"And your manager was fine with it."

"Because he knows we're professionals." He punches me in the shoulder, and I glare at him.

"What the fuck?"

"Just being bros." He laughs, and I flip him off because his bony ass knuckles probably left a bruise. "Come on."

I roll my eyes but follow him to the couch. My nerves hit me hard, but I try my best to get it all under control. When it's all set up and we go live, it's Grady who instantly goes into performance mode.

He smiles pretty for the camera and answers most of the questions which consist of easy ones like when we met and what we were like growing up. He easily sells the whole idea that we're childhood friends who played sports together and went out on double dates, which is pretty much true.

He left out the part where I watched him like a fucking creeper on those dates, wishing like hell he was holding my hand and not whatever chick he was on the date with.

It's apparent that I've been too quiet by the death glare Jenny is giving me, and I straighten when the host directs his question right at me. "So, are you happy to have your buddy back, Ryan? I mean, this has to be the greatest time in your life. Best friend back in town and winning the World Series?"

Is that really a question? My hands feel clammy, but I manage a nod. "Yeah. It's umm . . ." I look at Grady, who's trying like hell not to laugh at me and then back at the camera. "It really is the best time of my life. I'm just living on the high." I know they need a soundbite for their articles later.

The host lights up and nods, and I know he's thanking me for finally not being such a lame interviewee. "And what about you, Grady? What's next? Are you staying in KC for a bit?"

My stomach drops. Three weeks. Less than that now. That's all we really have. "For a couple of weeks, but then I start my US tour."

The audience cheers. "That's right. How long is that tour? And is it all of the US or are you just going to the cool parts?"

Grady easily chuckles at that, playing the game. "It's all over the US, and I think it's six months."

Six. Months. Motherfucker.

I'm sure I look sick, and I can feel the daggers Jenny's eyes are shooting at me, but I don't give a fuck. Six months? By then, I'll be back on the rigorous baseball schedule.

"Yeah, but then after that, who knows? Maybe I'll take a break for a bit."

He looks over at me briefly as the audience boos at the thought of him not being on tour where they can get a chance of seeing him. He raises his hands in mock surrender with a laugh only I know is forced.

"Well, hell. Maybe not."

The host does his job and laughs along. "Yeah, I don't think they're going to let you off that easy." The late night host looks to his audience. "But that's just because you love Immoral, right, guys?"

They hoot and holler, but I'm close to a breakdown. The host wraps it up, letting us go, and the camera crew cleans up, leaving my house the way they found it. But I can't shake the sick feeling, and I know Grady is feeling it too.

Unfortunately, a talk about it is going to have to wait because Waylon and Jenny—who have somehow become fast friends—have decided to order a late lunch/early dinner for us all.

Fuck, can't a man just be alone to wallow in self-pity for a bit?

GRADY

"Okay, that was fun and all, but I have a plane to catch." Jenny pushes her plate away from her and leans back in the chair where we're all sitting out on Ry's patio.

The fucked-up thing is, it was actually a fun meal. Jenny's not so bad when she slightly relaxes. And Waylon really seems to have taken a liking to her.

"I'll walk you out," Ry says as he stands up, tossing his napkin on the table. He, however, has been stiff and distant ever since the interview. I know what's bugging him. It's not hard to understand his freak-out because I'm freaking out about the same damn thing.

Six month tour.

Six months without Ry. Without being in his bed. Without kissing him. Without . . .

I try to stop my train of thought, considering Waylon is already eyeing me as he chugs his wine and pours some more. Guess he's taking an Uber back to his hotel tonight. "Out with it."

"Out with what?" I play coy, taking another drink.

"You two went for it, huh? You gonna give me all the dirty details?"

He waggles his eyebrows at me, and I toss my napkin at him. "Fuck off."

He laughs. "Clearly, you did it wrong, though, because your boy is awfully tense."

"Yeah. Well, you didn't help with your bullshit before the interview. What the fuck, Waylon?"

"Hey." He holds up his hands defensively. "I'm your manager first and foremost, and it was obvious to me that you've fucked. Just looking out for you."

I know he was, but it still sucked. "Well, you freaked him the hell out."

He studies me for a moment, and I hate when he does this. Waylon knows me pretty well. "You're really totally fine with all this, aren't you?"

I roll my eyes. "It's really not that big of a deal."

"Pretty sure it would be for most 'straight' people."

I shrug my shoulders and lean back into my chair. "Maybe I was never totally straight. Or maybe I truly don't give a fuck." My eyes move toward the glass door that leads into Ryan's house, and I see no sign of Ry. I turn back to Waylon. "Maybe it's just him. And always has been."

He clutches his heart, being an asshole. "That is the cutest thing."

"Fuck. Off." But I'm smiling.

He laughs. "Is he on board with this thought?"

He seemed pretty on board last night when my cock was in his ass, but I don't say that out loud. "I'm pretty sure."

A crease forms on his otherwise wrinkle-free forehead. "Pretty sure is not okay. You need to both be sure sure."

"What the fuck are you talking about? He's gay."

"He may be gay, but he's not out. And he's an athlete." This is nothing new to me, but Waylon continues, "Trust me on this, nothing hurts more than thinking someone loves you and you're on the same page, only to find out you weren't. Not at all."

That's cryptic as fuck. Especially for Waylon. "What the hell does that mean?"

He sighs heavily and looks out at the pool. "It means, you need to talk. Find out what you both want from this. Your world . . . if you guys are outed somehow, we could probably work around it. But his?" He shakes his head. "Trust me. His world is different."

"Pretty sure my label would freak the fuck out."

He chuckles at that and finishes off another drink. "No doubt. Please be careful, but still, I could spin it."

"We aren't planning anything. We're just . . ."

"Winging it? Playing it the Grady Bell way?"

Well fuck, that's creepy. "Were you watching us last night?"

He stands up from his seat, a little wobbly. "I wouldn't object to watching. But no. I just know you. Act first, think later. You can't do that."

I know he's right, but today has really fucked with my head enough already. "I know I want Ry. And I'll take him however I can get him."

That brings a surprised smile to his face. "Good. Be happy. Do your thing, and I'll run interference. But if you two decide to come out, please run it by me first."

"Promise."

He slaps my shoulder. "Time for me to go."

He starts to leave, but I have to ask. "Hey, Waylon?"

He turns toward me. "Yeah?"

"Did someone hurt you?"

He laughs, but it's sad and distant. "It was a long time ago. You know me." He forces a smile. "I always bounce back."

With that, he turns toward the door and heads inside to call his Uber. I want to know more because he's really the best friend I've had lately, but I don't want to pry. I saw the pain in his eyes. Clearly, he's been hurt by someone. Maybe someone he thought would come out for him and didn't. Nothing stings worse than betrayal.

I drag my hand over my jaw, feeling shaken and unsettled by the day.

Ryan and I definitely need to talk.

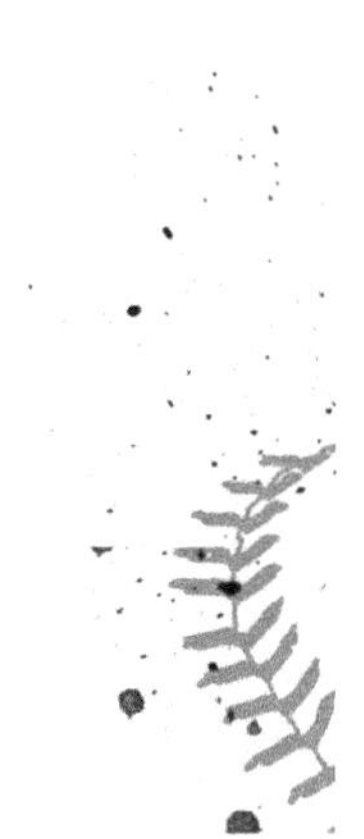

RYAN

"So, it's officially over with Vicky." I look up at the sound of Grady's voice. He's freshly showered and wearing only a pair of gray sweats that makes my fucking mouth water.

I'm drained after today. Jenny wasn't thrilled with my interview performance, but she doesn't seem to suspect that Grady and I are anything other than good friends. Thank fuck because I don't think I can take much more right now.

All I want to do is turn my mind off and get lost in Grady for the next three weeks. But I can't stop thinking about what happens after that. He's leaving for six months. Then, if I'm lucky enough to get a contract, I'll be on a crazy-ass traveling schedule myself after that.

I break through my thoughts to ask. "Oh, yeah?"

He sits next to me on my bed. "Yeah." He hands me his phone, and I see the headline immediately which states that Vicky is now dating a redhead who works at her local gym.

A female redhead. I look at him in surprise. "She's a lesbian?"

He nods. "Officially, she didn't know until she met this

woman. But unofficially, she's always known, and her show wasn't cool with it."

Motherfucker. This world just keeps getting better and better.

"*That's* why you dated her?"

He nods, putting his phone down and leaning back against my headboard. "They needed to clean up my image a bit, and Vicky . . . Well, the show thought she needed a boyfriend because people were getting suspicious."

"Suspicious that she was a lesbian?"

"I guess. I don't fucking know. I knew who she was even if I wasn't a fan of her show. Waylon approached me about a date with her. And before I knew it, we were in a fake relationship."

"So, how are you being portrayed in this whole thing?" Everything is fucking fake. I know that now. Without a doubt, his role in this is being spun by someone behind the scenes.

Puppets are all we are.

"The understanding ex who loved her but wants her to be happy. Happy she found her truth." His tone sounds as unhuman and dead as I've ever heard it.

I roll my eyes. "People will, no doubt, eat that shit up."

"Yeah, I can already hear the 'he really has changed' and 'aw, he's such a good man' commentary. His tone is bitter, and I can see how much he hates all this.

My hand smooths over his cheek as I turn to face him, my body angling toward his. "It's okay, Grady. At least she's free."

"I'm a fucking fraud."

I search his eyes and see how he, too, is drained from today. He's feeling it, and I kiss him softly, wanting to remind him we're in this together, even if I'm not sure for how long. He kisses me back, pushing my body back and moving his over me.

The kiss turns hungry. All I want to do is get lost in him and ignore the rest of the world, but I know we need to talk. "Grady . . ."

He shakes his head, but he pulls back to look at me. "We have to talk, don't we?"

"I think so."

His hand moves between our bodies, roaming over my bare chest and then down over my boxer briefs—the only thing I'm wearing. "Or we could talk later." His lips move to my neck, nipping and sucking softly. "I haven't been able to stop thinking about your ass all day."

I groan, my cock, already on its way to hard, is now like granite, pressing against his thigh. "Not fair."

He chuckles and then falls onto his back next to me. "Fine."

"How is this going to work? I mean, I like the Grady Bell method. But truly, how the fuck can it work? I'm not out. I doubt I'll be able to be out for a while. You're going on a six-month tour."

"And baseball is fucking insane with how much you travel."

"Exactly." I roll to my side. "So how?"

Instead of doing something impulsive like I'd expect, he seems to really think it over. I'm not sure if that makes me more or less uneasy. "I don't know. I really don't. But what I do know," his hand brushes over my arm, sending a thrill through me that I need to ignore for now, "is that I want this to work. However we have to make it work."

"I don't know if I can come out." I swallow the sickening truth. I'm sick of fucking hiding, but I don't know if I'm ready for the backlash or if I ever will be. "Even if I get a solid contract, I'm not naïve enough to believe it would all be just fine."

He looks angry but not at me. "I know. We don't have to do anything publicly."

"But won't that hurt? I mean, really think about it. It was hard for me not to touch you today during a live video. But never touching when we're out? Never? Just let the world think we're friends? How long before people grow suspicious?"

I sit up, throwing my legs over the edge of the bed and leaning into my hands, hunched over.

"Maybe we should just take these three weeks together." I drop my hands and look over my shoulder at Grady, who's moved behind me, sitting up. "I'd rather have three weeks with you than nothing."

"You can have more than that. You deserve more than that. We both deserve more."

"But it's impossible, and you know it. You're leaving for six months."

"I'll cancel it."

I snort and turn to face him fully. "Because that's not suspicious as fuck."

"I don't care." He doesn't crack a smile. He's dead serious, and I realize this has gone way too far.

I grab his face in my hands and lean my forehead against his. "I. Do. You love what you do. You can't give it up for me."

"I would."

"I know," I breathe and know I've had enough of the talking. This will probably end badly. There's really no good long-term fix for this, but I don't care. Right now, I have Grady in my bed, where I've always dreamed he'd be, and I'm not wasting a second.

I bring my lips to his and kiss him deeply, pulling a long groan from him as I push him back on the bed and cover his body with mine. My hands grasp his hair, intensifying the kiss, and we both move our bodies together in perfect unison.

His cock grinds against mine, the material too damn much and clearly frustrating the hell out of both of us. "Are you still sore?" He breathes the question, and I smile, shaking my head, not really knowing whether it's a lie but not giving a damn.

I grab a condom and lube, just needing him again and again. When we're both fully naked and his gorgeous dick is covered in latex, his mouth trails over my body, leaving light kisses everywhere.

I'm eager for him, and, not wanting to take it slow, I turn over, thrusting my ass up in the air. "Fuck me, Bell."

"Jesus, fuck." I feel his hands on my cheeks, pulling them apart and then hear another needy groan. "Fuck, I could come just from looking at you."

"Don't do that. I want you inside me." I feel the pad of his finger at my hole, and at this point, I'm desperate.

"I'm ready. Fuck. Me." I'm not really. I know that, but I don't fucking care.

I'm needy and wanting, my ass in the air, thrusting backward and seeking so much more. But when I feel his tongue circle my puckered hole, I fucking melt forward into the mattress onto my elbows. "Holy. Fuck."

He doesn't stop, rimming me and turning me into an even needier, fucking frenzied mess as his tongue breaches my hole, getting it nice and wet.

His finger joins his tongue, and I can't take it anymore. "Grady. Fuck me now, or I'm going to come."

Finally, I feel lube drizzle between my crack and his finger prodding my hole. First one, then two and three, stretching me. My voice is a pleading, incoherent mess. And then, fucking finally, his cock moves into me with short shallow thrusts until he's fully seated inside me, his front draped over my back. "Holy fuck."

"Move."

"I can't. I'll fucking come."

I smile, relishing in the full feeling, being totally invaded and stretched by his cock, but needing him to move. "I thought you weren't a chump."

His teeth nip my shoulder hard enough to leave a mark, but I only grin, knowing I hit his competitive nerve. "You know I'm not. Give me a second, fucker. You feel so goddamn good."

"So do you." I reach behind me, grabbing his hip. "Now show me how good you can really feel."

He pulls back, and I brace myself before he thrusts back into me, deep inside my ass, hitting my prostate and making lightning shoot up my spine.

"Yes. That's fucking it. Use that big cock."

"Jesus, you're bossy." But he does it again, at the exact same, perfect angle that hits my gland and makes my dick leak from the tip as I thrust into the mattress.

"You love it."

"I do." My hand moves from his hip to my cock, using the precum as lube to slide along my shaft, chasing my release. His hands grasp my hips, pulling my body into his as he thrusts deep inside me. "Fuck. Fuck. Fuck," he chants, and I know he's as close as I am.

"Yes." My hand slides over my cock furiously. "I'm close."

"Please come, Ry. I can't take much more."

That's apparently all I needed because cum shoots from my dick onto the sheets below, and I feel his cock throb in my ass before he lets out a guttural moan I feel throughout my entire body.

His body collapses onto mine, and I don't even care that I'm smashed between him and a sticky mattress. He feels too fucking good.

Everything feels way too fucking good.
For right now.

GRADY

OKAY, so we haven't solved a goddamn thing, but I don't care. Right now, I just can't bring myself to care that we haven't defined shit.

I know I want him. I know he wants me. And for the past week, we've just been enjoying that fact. Because right now, that's all we need.

We've kept it low-key, mostly just hanging out at Ryan's house. We did manage to sneak out and get tested. I'm happy as fuck the results are back. His came in yesterday, and he's totally clean. I just got the email that I'm good to go, and now, I'm waiting for Ry, who decided he needed to go pick up our food instead of having it delivered today.

The anticipation is killing me, but I'm ready for this. I'm ready to have all of him. When Ry gets back with the food, I'm on him at the door in an instant. My hand steals the food away from him and drops the paper bag to the floor as my lips trail over his neck. "Guess what?"

At that point, I realize he's stiff and not kissing me back. When I pull back enough to look at his face, I see how pale he is.

"Ry? What's wrong?"

"Umm . . ." His voice is strained as he places his keys on the table and picks up the bag of food from the ground, aimlessly walking toward the kitchen.

"Ry, you're fucking scaring me. What happened?"

"I heard something on the radio." He places the bag on the counter, and I reach for his hand, stopping him from going any further without telling me what the fuck is going on.

"What?"

His eyes finally lift, and I see sympathy in them. "Your dad . . ."

"What the fuck did he do now?" My hands are shaking. That motherfucker always brings out the worst reactions from me. *Did he somehow find out about Ryan and me?*

He reaches for his phone and then holds it up, showing me a picture of my father's congregation members posed outside a mansion I know to be Vicky's.

"That motherfucker."

"Apparently, they didn't like the news of his son's girlfriend now dating a woman."

I take a seat on the barstool conveniently placed at the counter island. "Of course, he wouldn't." I look at the headline, which states very clearly that the church's leader is my father. "Fuck. They know."

"How the hell did you keep this shit under wraps for so long?"

I run my fingers through my hair. "I don't know. I really don't. But I thought maybe, just maybe, my father would care so little about me, he'd just let me go."

I feel Ry's strong arms embrace me from behind. "I'm sorry."

"I need to call Vicky. Apologize. No one knows about this part of my life."

"Not even Waylon?" Ry's pointing at something, and I realize it's the security cam. Sure enough, right on time, Waylon is at the gate.

"Fuck. No. Not even him."

Ry buzzes him in, and we wait out front for him as his car flies up toward the house and parks before Waylon climbs out and is coming in hot. "Seriously. That fucking psycho is your dad?"

"Yes." Hot shame spreads through me. "That's my father."

"How could you not tell me that?"

I shrug, except I'm anything but nonchalant. I feel like shit just for having been born that man's son. "It's not something I'm proud of. It's something I wanted buried."

"We should probably go inside." Ry opens the front door. "Who knows who's watching."

Waylon and I don't argue, all of us heading into Ryan's living room to sit down, but it's Ry who speaks to Waylon before I can. "His father is a piece of shit, but as you can see, he's gained a lot of followers, all spreading hate under the pretense of love."

Waylon looks sick, and I can't blame him. He's spent his life fighting against people like my father and not just in his own life. He's been an ally to so many and frequently volunteers with gay youths, trying to strengthen them. People like my father only threaten to undo all the good he's done.

"How can you be related to him?"

Ry wraps his big arm around my shoulder. "I ask myself that all the time. But you know him, he's nothing like his father."

Although I appreciate it, it still makes me cringe. People have told me my entire life I'm the spitting image of my father.

"I know that." Waylon's eyes seem sympathetic. "Why didn't you tell me?"

"I was ashamed. I just wanted him to go the fuck away."

He nods as if he understands. "You have the same last name? How am I only finding out about this?"

"I wanted to change my name. But the record label loved Bell, so they made me keep it. Said they could handle it."

"They know?" Ryan seems surprised. Why, I'm not sure. He knows the game. They dug every single thing up about me before signing me.

Before I can answer, Waylon is turning on the television and immediately finding news coverage of the church gathering outside Vicky's home. Thank God for the iron gate around her property, but it's still unnerving.

These people are seriously psychotic. Last year, one of my father's minions went to prison for bombing an abortion clinic. The year before that, the fuckers attacked a veteran who just got back from serving our country they claim to love.

"Clearly they can't handle it."

I don't see Vicky, so she must be inside, probably scared out of her mind. "I need to call Vicky." I stand up to reach into my pocket for my cell, but Waylon stops me.

"She's fine."

"How do you know?" I gesture toward the TV, my stomach dropping at the signs these people are holding up with sickening, hateful words.

"She's on her way to an undisclosed location with her girlfriend for a few weeks. These assholes will get bored and move on soon enough."

I sit back down and look up at him in surprise. "How do you know that?"

He waves me off, plopping down in one of Ry's oversized chairs. "Please. I was way ahead of this shit. I just didn't know he was your fucking father."

Of course, he was ahead of it. Waylon is beyond amazing at his job. "I'm sorry. I should have told you."

"I get not wanting to be associated with him, Grady . . . But what the hell?"

"I didn't want you to see me as part of him." I feel Ry's big hand on the back of my neck giving me a reassuring massage that I welcome. "I hate him."

Waylon offers a sympathetic smile yet again. "Me too. But I know that's not you. You aren't your father."

"I've let him take a lot of shit from me." I look over at Ry's solemn face, and I know he knows I mean him. If it weren't for that asshole, maybe I would have tried harder to track down Ry a long time ago. I would have faced shit I'd buried.

"Well, if anything, people are only going to sympathize with you. I mean, with a father like that? You turned out pretty damn well."

"Thanks, Waylon."

"No more fucking secrets. I swear to God, if you have a love child somewhere you aren't telling me about, I will kill you."

"Me too," Ry adds, and it actually makes me relax into him and laugh.

"Are you sure Vicky is okay?"

Waylon nods. "She's okay. Really. She was worried about you."

Of course, she was. I'm not sure how I got so goddamn lucky to have such good people in my life when honestly, I was doomed from the start. I could be like the rest of my family, blindly following my father and believing his bullshit lies.

I lean on Ry and smile to myself.

Growing up, I had him to commiserate with and question the shit my father was spewing.

If I didn't have that, maybe I would have been lost in that world.

RYAN

IT'S BEEN a couple of days since the shit show with Grady's father. He's been in his head over it, which is a strange switch of roles. But I get it. God, do I get it. I'll never forget being forced to sit in the front pew with my parents and listen to the hateful shit coming out of his father's mouth.

And his parishioners shouting a resounding "amen."

Grady and I would sit there solemnly, silently mocking all the ignorant bastards, but it still gets to you. It still gets deep inside your subconscious, and I know he worries there's an ugly side to him.

If only he knew—he's beautiful, inside and out. Always has been.

"Vicky is somewhere tropical." He smiles, showing me a pic on his phone of Vicky in a bikini with her beautiful girlfriend leaning on her shoulder.

"She looks happy."

He nods, putting his phone on the side table next to the sofa, running his fingers through his hair. "Yeah. Thank fuck."

"It's not your fault, Grady."

"What if they'd been attacked, Ry? For being gay. What the fuck is wrong with this world?"

"A lot." I move closer to him, pressing a kiss to his temple. "But there's good too."

"How can you say that? With all you've had to deal with?"

I don't like this side of Grady—not because it's not as fun or because I want light and carefree—but because that truly is Grady's personality. It's not a front. He lives life to the fullest. He has a good time and can usually spin everything into good.

I'm the grumpy bastard.

I brush a kiss against his lips and smile as I remain there. "You make it good. You show me the good. Always have."

He finally grins, and now, things feel right again. "You've always been good for me too. I hated my father, but you made it okay to be happy."

"I think I can make you really, really happy right now." I waggle my eyebrows at him, and he snorts, shoving me back but not far. He lifts his shirt off, tossing it behind him, and I do the same, not wanting to waste any more time.

I practically growl when he pulls his sweatpants down, his cock hard and slapping against his abs. "Fuck." I'm starving for him.

The last two nights he's slept in my bed, but other than a few kisses here and there, there hasn't been much physical activity.

Which I'm cool with, but this is more like it.

I let my fingers slide over his abs, my mouth following as I leave a trail with my tongue. "What do you want, Grady?"

"You." His hand slides through my hair, and I smile like an idiot.

"You have me. What do you want me to do?"

"Stop talking and use that mouth to suck my cock." His fingers grasp my hair tighter as he gets bossier, and I groan, leaning down to lick the tip, teasing and making his hips buck upward impatiently. "I said suck, not lick."

"You don't like my tongue?" I run it along the vein on the underside of his dick, and he moans.

"Fuck. I do. I really do." I smile, putting him out of his misery and engulfing his shaft, cupping his balls, and loving his moans of ecstasy, knowing he's right on the edge.

Of course, that's when my nosey-as-fuck agent with zero boundaries decides to burst into my home.

Because why the hell not ten minutes ago? Or an hour from now? No, it had to be with Grady nearly naked on my couch and his cock deep in my throat.

"Are you fucking kidding me?"

I pull away from Grady, not wanting to, but he tugs his sweats up over his ass and stands, glaring over the couch at Jenny. "You have the worst fucking timing. Anyone ever tell you that?"

She doesn't flinch, just walks closer. "You're supposed to be fucking straight. How was I supposed to know you two would be playing a new little game in the middle of the afternoon?"

I sit up, not pulling my shirt on. "Why are you here?"

She puts a hand on her hip, raising her perfectly manicured eyebrow. "Why the hell did you have your best friend's dick in your mouth?"

I'm guessing she doesn't want to hear *"because I wanted him to come down my throat,"* so I stay silent.

Grady, on the other hand, must be feeling back to his normal self because he smirks at her and answers, "Because it's a fantastic dick. Duh. And he really knows what he's doing."

She rolls her eyes, and I fight a laugh. This is why he's my best friend. She walks to a chair and slumps down, looking pretty damn defeated for her. "Your contract is already in danger, and now this. Are you trying to kill me? I'm thirty. Too young to have a fucking stroke."

"You can have a stroke at any age," Grady offers, not helping.

She glares at him, but I intercept, "What do you mean my contract is in danger? What now?"

She leans forward. "You and Bennett are considered a package deal, but lately, he's been floating the idea that he wants to move to the West Coast."

"He wouldn't do that." I turn my body so I'm facing her, on high alert now.

"His wife's family is there, and they're starting their own family. She wants to be near them."

Grady looks concerned, but he doesn't say anything. "He's never said anything to me. He wouldn't do that. He loves it here. He loves the fans. They stuck by us when we fucking sucked."

"I know." She sighs, seemingly having lost all fight, which is just not good. "But I don't think it's a rumor, and it's affecting the negotiations. It puts your contract at risk."

"They would be stupid not to keep Ry." Grady's voice is a low, defensive growl.

"I agree." Her eyes meet his. "But it doesn't mean they won't let him go without Bennett. Or pay him far less."

"Then I'll walk."

She sighs. "You really want to walk away from here?"

I don't know. It's where I started. It's close to everything I know, but maybe they'd be more accepting of me out west. Who the fuck knows?

"I don't know."

She nods her head, already knowing my answer before I

said it. She waves her arm in our direction, "And now this? You're fucking Grady Bell? Seriously?"

Again, Grady goes on the defense. "And what's wrong with that? You already know he's gay."

"I know he goes to clubs occasionally with a hat and sunglasses and selects a cute twink who'll sign an NDA and who he'll never see again. Fucking his best friend that the whole country has eyes on? Not great."

I bristle, hating that she's right about this being far more dangerous. "We'll be careful," Grady insists.

And he gets another famous Jenny eye roll. "It's really only a matter of time before this comes out." She throws her hands in the air as she stands. "I can't believe I didn't see this before. I'm getting soft."

Grady snorts, "This is you soft? Jesus."

She flips him off, and I stand up between them. "Stop. Both of you." I aim my look at Jenny. "We'll be careful."

"The meeting is coming up. Can you keep this a secret until then, at least?"

"I've been doing it all this time."

She doesn't look convinced but takes a deep breath. "I'll be in touch."

She starts for the door, and Grady turns around, looking over the back of the couch. "Yeah, maybe you should start knocking. Unless you want to see a lot more of my dick."

"Not helping," I say in his direction but can't fight the smile on my face.

He winks, and I shake my head, ushering Jenny outside and saying a quick goodbye before walking to the patio door and looking outside, grateful for the large yard and the fence that surrounds it. It gives me the illusion of privacy, at least.

I feel Grady's body crowding mine from behind. "It's going to be okay."

"Is it?" I don't turn around, back to being the one in his head. I can't believe Bennett did that shit without at least talking to me first.

But I give him the benefit of the doubt. Not like there isn't a hell of a lot he doesn't know about me.

His mouth is on my neck now, leaving sweet kisses. "I bet I know what can make you feel better . . ."

I roll my eyes. "Sex can't fix everything."

"No, but it can't hurt."

I laugh and turn to face him. "Your balls as blue as mine?"

He groans and leans his forehead against mine. "Probably bluer. I mean, your mouth was sending me straight to heaven when Jen-nay had to burst in here and ruin it."

I laugh, "She fucking hates when you pronounce her name like that, but I think I can finish what I started."

He shakes his head, surprising me. "I was thinking of something different." I quirk an eyebrow, and his mouth moves to my ear. "I was thinking you could fuck me."

My mouth is suddenly dry as I try my best to swallow. He pulls back and looks into my eyes. "I want that."

He grins and grabs my hand, leading me to my room.

I guess he wants that too.

GRADY

OKAY, don't be nervous. It's just a dick. A long, thick dick going into my ass, but still.

"Breathe." I look at Ry who has an amused smirk on his gorgeous, all-American face.

"I am breathing."

His hand moves over my heart. We're both naked and standing at the foot of the bed, staring at each other because I fucking froze. Even though this was my idea in the first place. "Jesus, your heart is racing."

Yeah. Yeah, it is. I let out a shaky breath and run my fingers through my hair. "Maybe I'm a little nervous."

He doesn't mock me, just brings his mouth to my neck, kissing softly and dragging his lips up to my earlobe, nibbling ever so slightly. "We don't have to do this. I'm fine with you doing all the fucking."

I don't want that though. I want to know what it feels like to be completely owned by Ryan. To give him this part of me. "No. I want this."

I wish my voice portrayed even a little bit of confidence. Fuck. I'm not used to this. He studies me closely, pulling back to look at my face as his hands slide over my abs. "If you hate it, say stop. We don't ever have to do it again."

And I know he means it. I know he won't hold it against me either. Because that's just Ry. "I want to give it a chance." My hands move to his hips, pulling him to me. His cock is hard and pressing against me. My nerves have gotten to me, leaving me with only a semi.

He nods in a calm, reassuring way. "Okay. Do you want me to use a condom?"

"Fuck no." My answer is instant, which makes him laugh. "Just you." I kiss him softly. The kiss quickly moves into passionate and hungry desire, and we end up on the bed with his solidly muscular body on top of me.

His mouth is magic as it trails over my jaw to my throat, licking at my Adam's apple and making me groan in anticipation. For a while, he teases my nipples that are surprisingly sensitive, sucking, licking and biting until I'm a writhing desperate mess.

"Fuck, Ry."

I feel him smile as he moves lower over my stomach and then urges me to bend my knees, leaving my feet flat on the bed and opening myself to him in the most intimate way I can imagine. My cock is up and ready to play again, especially when he tongues my balls and goes lower, lower, lower until he's at my hole. He spends time there, getting me wet and ready for him, sending zings of pleasure throughout my body with each lash of his tongue.

"Yes," I gasp, my hands grasping his hair.

"I can't wait to be inside you, Grady."

"Only you, Ry."

He moans against me, sending more thrill through my

thrumming body. When he grabs the lube and slicks his finger, he looks up at me as if waiting for approval. I give him a quick nod even though I feel the nerves returning.

We've done this before. I've enjoyed it, especially when he finds the spongy spot inside me that brought me to the closest thing to what I'd consider the existence of God because, holy fuck, everything goes bright white.

His mouth engulfs my cock, somehow nearly taking all of it in as he works one finger inside and then two, hitting said spot expertly and making me curse and mumble incoherent words. "You're going to make me come."

He releases my dick and looks up at me with a wicked grin. "And that would be a bad thing?"

I nod, barely getting the words out when he tongues the tip of my cock, teasing the fuck out of me. "When your cock isn't inside me? Yeah."

He groans and withdraws his fingers, climbing up my body to meet my lips with his. We kiss for a while, our cocks rubbing against each other until I can't take it anymore.

"Fuck me, Ry."

His head rests against mine and even though he's holding most of his weight off me, I feel his body everywhere. I feel him, heart, body, and soul, and I know I want him inside me.

"Are you sure?"

I nod my consent even if I can't seem to get the words out. His lips meet mine again reverently as if he's telling me it'll be everything I need it to be, and I believe him.

I reach for the lube, slicking up his cock before allowing him to take it and drizzle even more of it onto my hole, pushing some of it inside with his fingers. I close my eyes, letting it feel good.

"I'm ready," I manage to say as he drops the lube next to us and lines up his thick cock at my entrance. I feel myself tense as he presses ever so slightly.

He shakes his head. "Don't tense up. Relax. Breathe."

I try my best, but my breath comes out shaky. "Just do it. I'll be fine."

He shakes his head again. "No. I'm not going to hurt you."

"I'm fine. Don't be a pussy and fuck me already." The false bravado doesn't work on Ry though.

Of course, it doesn't. Instead, his hand reaches between us, finding my cock that's starting to wilt with nerves. He strokes me, looking into my eyes before he kisses me, and I relax slightly into him.

After a while, I feel him pressing inside me, past that first ring of muscle, and it slightly burns, the intrusion uncomfortable, but I don't want him to stop.

He doesn't ask me, thank God. He must know instinctively I don't want him to. I want to do this. I don't back down from anything, and I'm not about to start now. He slowly inches into my body, kissing me and stroking my dick that's starting to gain more and more interest. I take his advice and breathe through it.

Once he's fully seated inside me, he somehow manages not to move a muscle as he pulls his head back and meets my eyes. I can see the unadulterated pleasure on his face—enough to make me want to do this because goddamn, he's beautiful. "God, Grady. You feel so fucking good."

"I think it would feel even better if you were moving."

He laughs lightly, his eyes closing, and I notice the veins in his neck pulled tight with tension. "I'm trying to give you time to adjust, you jackass."

I feel full and oddly satisfied that I did this. I managed to let him inside me. I'm the reason for that blissed-out expression on his face. "Move, Ry. I can take it. Fuck me."

A strangled groan leaves his lips as he leans back, grabbing my thighs and parting them more. Then he pulls back, his cock nearly leaving me and thrusts inside but not hard. Not like I'm sure he's dying to do. No, he's still gentle as he glides inside me, adjusting his angle. When his cock hits that magical spot deep inside me, my cock jumps back into action, leaking from the tip. I gasp, "Ry, there."

He smirks, like he knew exactly what he just did. And knowing this fucker, he does. He pegs that spot over and over, sending me to nirvana.

I thought this first time would be about his pleasure and was totally fine with that. Hoping he would get off fast and then maybe the next time we tried, it would get better, but that's just not Ryan Bailey's style. No, this fucker has to go for the championship with everything he does.

"Yes," I gasp again, shocked at how hard my cock is and how close I am to losing it just from his dick being inside me.

"Are you going to come for me, Grady?"

"I want to." I feel desperate and unsure of what I need, but Ry knows, he just knows. When his hand wraps around my cock, stroking it with a firm hand, I nearly lose it. "Oh fuck, tell me you're close."

"Are you kidding? I nearly came the second I was inside you. You feel fucking perfect." He's a sight to be seen. Solid muscle and beauty, everything pulled tight with lust and pleasure-filled tension.

"Come, Ry."

"You first." He thrusts inside me at the perfect angle,

simultaneously stroking my cock, his thumb playing with my tip. I don't even get a chance to argue before I shoot hot cum all over my abs.

"Fuck," he chokes out as he thrusts only a couple of strokes before I feel his cock pulse inside me. "Fuck."

I can't find words, but I silently agree with him.

Holy fucking shit. How the hell have I been living without this all these years?

When we finally regain some of our wits, we decide to take a shower to clean up. I don't want to be too far away from him, feeling oddly vulnerable. And he seems to understand that too, turning on only one showerhead and keeping his large body against mine as we wash each other off.

"I don't want to leave," I admit when his strong arms wrap around me from behind, and we both let the water pour over the top of us.

"I don't want you to leave either. But we'll be okay. We'll get through this."

I smile sadly as I lean against the tile shower and let his body cloak mine. "Bailey and Bell."

"Bell and Bailey," he whispers against my ear. "Always."

I turn to face him, my heart thundering. "I want that, Ry. Forever."

"I want it too. Forever."

"Just me and you?"

He nods. "It's always been you for me."

My hand slides through his wet hair, my chest exploding with so much emotion I'd normally make a joke to avoid it, but not now. "You've always been it for me too. So, this is a thing? You and me? No one else?"

"No one else. I only want you."

I kiss him softly. "I only want you too." Because it needed to be said. Even if no one else was on my radar. I can't imagine being with anyone else after knowing his touch, and I want him to hear it out loud from me. "Exclusive couple then?"

He doesn't tease me about being an emotional mess or needing a definition, which is usually his thing. His forehead rests against mine, and his voice is firm and confident. "For the rest of my life, that's all I want."

And even though I'm leaving for a six-month tour and then his schedule is going to get insane, I've never felt more safe and secure in my life.

Because I know Ryan is mine.

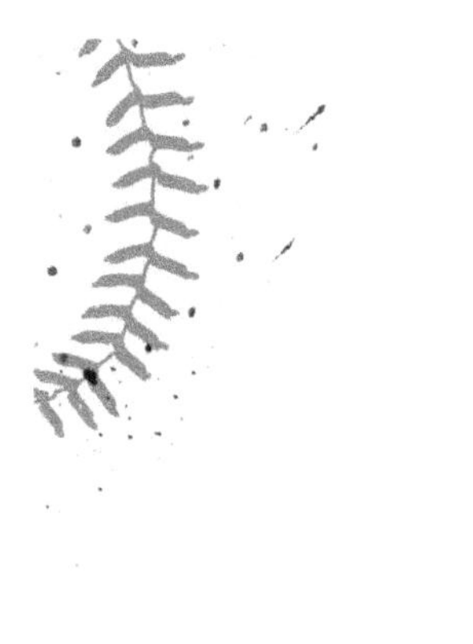

RYAN

"Fuck, I'm going to miss you." I hold Grady's body to mine in the foyer of my house because we can't say goodbye in an airport. No. I have to say it behind a closed door.

The bitterness in my gut turns but I try to stay strong for him. "I'm going to miss you too, Grady, but we can get through this."

"When is the big meeting?"

"Two days." Jenny sent me a text this morning, reminding me to be good.

There's been no drama since the day she busted us, and we've spent the entire time in our perfect bubble. Fucking and talking. Enjoying every single second of each other. But it wasn't enough. Not nearly enough.

This is all I fucking want.

Would I miss baseball if I couldn't play anymore? Sure.

But this? Letting the man I love go? Yeah, this might fucking kill me.

He looks nervous as he brushes a kiss over my lips and whispers, "I love you."

My heart aches, clenching tightly in my chest because I

know he means it. He's in love with me just as much as I'm in love with him, and we can't tell the world because it's full of too much hatred to accept our love.

"I love you too. God, I love you."

He kisses me hard, his hands on the sides of my face. "I'll call you every day."

I nod in agreement. "You fucking better."

He smiles. "The contract will go fine. They'd be fucking idiots not to keep you."

But do I even want that?

I stay tight-lipped and nod, but he doesn't let it pass. Pulling back so he can look into my eyes and holding onto my face with his big hands, he says, "You were made to play ball. You're too fucking good at it to let anything else get in the way."

"You're not just anything, Grady. You're everything."

He smiles, and I can see my admission makes him happy. "You don't have to worry about me. I'm not going anywhere, no matter what. We tell everyone tomorrow . . . I'm fine with that. We keep it our secret until your knees are all creaky, and you can't be on the catcher's mound anymore, and I'm a sweating gasping mess every time I'm on stage because I can't keep up . . . I'm fine with that too."

"That's a sexy picture you paint."

He chuckles, "I fucking love you. And don't worry about any of this shit. You and me, we're solid."

"Yeah, we are."

"Get the best fucking contract you possibly can. Everything else will fall right into place. You'll see."

Same ole Grady. I kiss him hard and then grab his hand "Let's get your ass to the airport."

It's a quiet, solemn ride to the airport, and when it's time for him to leave, we have to settle for a quick bro-hug because there are cameras watching.

It fucking sucks and doesn't sit right with me, but he leaves with the promise of so much more in the future.

And for now, that has to be okay.

That is, until later that day when I get a call from Jenny telling me the contract negotiations have been pushed back for another fucking two weeks.

God. Damn. It.

When Grady texts me that he's landed and is in his hotel room, I immediately call him. He answers right away. "Hey, miss me that much already?"

Yes. "How was your flight?" I try, but my voice is shaky, and it must alert him.

"What's wrong?"

I don't bother being coy. "Two more weeks, Grady. They pushed the negotiations back for two more fucking weeks. My future continues to hang in the balance."

"Well. Fuck."

"Yeah." I lean my head back against the couch, wishing like hell he was here, sitting next to me instead of a thousand miles away."

"It'll be okay, Ry." He sighs, and I hear his uncertainty.

"Jenny thinks it's because of Bennett."

"Have you talked to him?"

I haven't talked to him since the party, which is pretty shitty considering he's been the closest thing I've had to a best friend the last few years. "No."

"You should."

I smile, trying to make the conversation lighter even though I feel like shit. "I've been kind of busy."

He laughs, and I miss the hell out of that laugh, out of this man. "Yeah well, I'm not going to apologize for that, but you should go talk to him."

"I can't fault him for wanting what his wife wants to make her happy."

I can hear him smiling. "You should still talk to him. Maybe you could even tell him—"

I cut him off, "I don't know if I can do that." I sigh. "Maybe I should take my chances with another team."

"You love it there." I do. It's what I know, but maybe I'm ready for a change.

"I think I could love it somewhere else. Maybe I can find somewhere I can be open and free, Grady. We both know, contract or not, it probably won't go over so well in middle America."

"Fuck that shit. If you lock in a contract, you can do whatever the fuck you want."

He says it, but I'm not sure even he believes it. We know how the world works. How, if the fans aren't happy, the owners can find a way around any contract. "Yeah."

It's all I can manage to say. All I want is him here and in my arms when I feel so unsteady and out of control, but at least I have him on the phone.

At least I know, without a doubt, that no matter where he is in the world, he's mine.

And yeah, that's more than enough for me.

RYAN

"WELL HOLY SHIT, I was sure you were done with my ass." Bennett's smile is vibrant as he opens the door to his home and lets me inside. I decided Grady was right and I needed to talk to my friend and teammate.

So, after a couple of days of sulking, I gave him a call and asked if we could get together. He, of course, told me to come on over.

"Where's the wife?" I ask, caring about his wife as much as him. She's always been so fucking kind to me, and I do want her to be happy.

"She went baby stuff shopping with her mom. Come on in." He directs me to his man cave downstairs where he has a pool table, several recliners, and a big screen television with baseball highlights already on.

I laugh as I take a seat. "I can't believe she lets you have this place."

He chuckles. "Hey, she gets to decorate the rest of the house however she wants. I get to have this one thing."

I laugh again, and I realize I've missed Bennett. He's easygoing and always reminded me of Grady in some ways.

The 100 percent platonic type of ways. Never once did I pine after my teammate.

"So, what's up?" He takes a seat in the chair next to mine, and I decide to just grow a pair and say what's on my mind.

"You may not want to stay in KC, from what I hear."

He looks slightly guilty now, and I feel like an asshole. He deserves happiness. Who am I to take that away from anyone else? Especially knowing the sting of never quite getting what I want. He rubs the back of his neck, a sheepish look on his face. "I'm sorry, Ryan. I should have told you."

"So, it's true? You've been trying to negotiate with other teams?"

"Quietly. They were supposed to do it quietly and not let KC know about it, but of course, some jackass let it slip."

I try not to feel hurt. "But you didn't tell me?"

"I'm sorry, Ry. I really am. I don't even know what I want at this point." He looks stressed, and I know that feeling, so I stop him before he can say anything else.

"You want your wife to be happy. You want her to be able to be around her family when your kid is born. I get that."

He looks almost relieved. "I should have known you would. Still, I hate the idea of leaving behind the fans who have supported us this whole time. And you."

"Aw, you're going to miss me?" I kid, but he nods his head seriously.

"Yeah. We're a good team." His lanky shoulder shrugs. "Maybe we could still be a package deal somewhere on the West Coast?"

My heart flips, thinking about being on the same coast as Grady, but I also feel sick about leaving this town behind. "I don't know. It might be too late for all that."

"I'm not sure. Will you just think about it?"

I see the hope in his eyes, and fuck, I want to tell him everything. I want to tell him I'm gay and in love with my best friend. That might not be so bad for me, but I can't. I can't get my mouth to say the words.

"You never know."

He smiles and then grabs us both a beer, settling into an easy afternoon, like old times.

When I get home that night, I video call Grady, and when he answers the phone and I see his face with that goddamn grin on it, everything feels right again. "Hey."

"Hey, you okay?"

I force a smile and lean back into the couch I'm sitting on. "I went to Bennett's today."

I can't see much behind him, but I think he's on a hotel bed. He's wearing a tight black t-shirt, and that's all the detail I can see. "How did that go?"

"I couldn't tell him about me."

He doesn't look disappointed. "Is that why you went there?"

I shrug, holding the phone up and focusing on him. "I don't know. I wanted to talk to him about the contract, but I thought maybe I could finally tell him."

"So, why didn't you?"

I'm not ashamed of being gay, not in the slightest. I'm proud of who I am. And it may seem like I'm ashamed the way I've had to hide it, but if I didn't play baseball for a living, I'd, without a doubt, definitely be out and proud. "I couldn't make him keep that secret for me."

He smiles and nods his head in understanding. "So, not because you think he would act differently?"

"No. I think he would be fine with it, but keeping this secret . . . it's a lot to ask of anyone."

"Yeah. Yeah, it is. Too fucking much. You shouldn't have to keep it a secret."

There he goes, getting all protective. "Tell me about your concert last night."

"It was good. Full crowd. Receptive. But I fucking missed you."

That should make me smile, but all I feel is melancholy because I fucking miss him too. "I hate this."

"Hey, I was thinking. You have two more free weeks, right? You wanna come hang out with me on tour?"

"For two weeks?"

He runs a hand through his thick hair, looking adorably nervous. "Or a week. Or a couple of days. I don't know. I'd kill for any time with you."

Now, I'm smiling like an idiot. "Yeah. Where to next?"

"I fly into Philly tomorrow."

"I'll buy a ticket tonight."

His smile, beaming and excited, full of lust and love. And yeah, that's enough to make everything okay.

GRADY

THIS IS RIDICULOUS.

He's here, and I can't contain myself, but I know I have to reel it in. "Hey." I give him a half-bro-type hug when I want to kiss the fuck out of him. It's only been a few days, but my entire body is thrumming with excitement to see him.

He's in jeans and a plain tee with a baseball cap pulled low. "Hi."

I release him and step back much sooner than I want to. "Where to?"

"My hotel to check in." I try not to let my face fall, but he notices instantly, keeping his voice low. "Relax, I'm staying in your bed tonight. But in case anyone checks, I have my own room."

I smile and nod, noting there at least five people with cameras aimed our way. "Okay, sounds good."

I lead him to the car, both of us climbing in the back, and I direct the driver where to go. He checks into his room at the front desk, and then we go up to the room, deciding not to let it be a total waste.

When the door closes behind us, we don't lose anytime,

undressing in record time and letting our clothes fall wherever. We don't make it to the bed, though, kissing and grinding against each other, his back pressed against the wall.

"Fuck, I missed you."

I moan against his mouth, having missed his body being pressed against mine. "I missed you too. So goddamn much."

How the hell are we going to make it for six more months? When he can't get away like this? I try to shake that thought from my head. I'd rather think we can always find time to sneak away for each other.

His hand grasps my hard cock, stroking it, and when I do the same to him, his head meets the wall, tilting back and exposing his throat. I take full advantage, sucking and biting along the column. "I'm not going to last."

"We have plenty of time later." My hand moves faster, loving the feel of him in my grip. When he pushes my hand away from him, using his spit to lubricate his hand and wrapping it around both of us, I thrust against him, bracing myself on the wall with both hands.

"Fuck, Ry."

"Come with me, Grady."

It doesn't take long before we're both exploding with ecstasy, cum spilling over his hand and both of us groaning with spent desire. "Jesus. Fuck. I really, really missed you," I say with a smile that makes him laugh and then kiss me.

"I missed you too, asshole."

"Apparently." We both take a shower in the hotel bathroom that isn't anywhere near the luxury of his house, but it gets the job done.

When we're both cleaned and dressed again, we're ready to

head out for dinner when his phone rings. He checks it and curses, "Shit. It's my mom."

I take a seat on the edge of the bed. "Better answer it."

He sighs and takes a seat next to me, answering it and putting it on speaker phone. "Hey, Mom."

"Hi, sweetie. What are you up to?"

I offer him a wicked grin, challenging him to answer that honestly after what we just did, and he shakes his head with a laugh. "Hanging with Grady."

"Grady Bell?" She sounds so excited.

"Yeah, the one and only."

I greet her, "Hey, Mrs. Bailey."

"Oh, sweetie! How are you? We've missed seeing you around town. I'm so happy you and Ryan are friends again."

I see the shame on his face, and I don't like it. I don't let him get by with it for long. We were both responsible for our time apart. "Me too, Mrs. Bailey. He's not getting rid of me this time."

"I'm so happy to hear that! How are you these days? I've asked your father about you a couple of times. But you know him, he doesn't say much." I cringe at the thought of my father.

"Yeah, sounds like him. I'm fine, thank you."

Ryan gives me a cautious look, knowing how much my father bothers me, but his mother either doesn't notice or doesn't care and continues, "Well, I'm sure he's extremely proud of you like we are of Ryan."

Right, except for ignoring the fact that he's gay. Ry gives me a pleading look, and I comply, keeping my mouth shut even if it grates on me. "Right."

She switches her focus to Ryan. "Ryan, we heard the contract negotiations have been pushed back. What happened?"

Fuck. My plan was to keep his mind off that shit this week.

"It'll be fine, Mom."

"Oh, honey, I hope so." I can see the stress rolling off Ry in waves now, and I'm pissed because I just worked really hard to relieve his tension. Not that it was a hardship. "You just have to stay here."

"Yeah, that's the plan." He sounds resigned.

"But if not, you know someone will want him, and they'll be the luckiest team in the world." I add, trying to get her to shut up.

It doesn't work. "No. There's no other team for Ryan. He needs to be here. Near his family and in the town that loves him."

The town that makes him hide who he really is.

I'm pretty sure I'm tasting blood from biting my tongue so damn hard.

"It'll be fine, Mom. I'll call you when I know more, okay?"

"Okay, sweetie. I'll pray for you. We love you."

"Love you too. Tell Dad hi."

They hang up, and Ry lies flat on his back, covering his face with his hand, the phone next to him on the bed.

"You okay?" I lie down next to him.

"I'm fine. Should have known it would be news that my contract is in danger."

"Yeah well, they'd be fucking stupid to let you go. You just won the World Series, Ry. You have a pretty big bargaining chip."

"Not without Bennett. Not for the price we're trying for."

I don't think he's that concerned about the money, but no doubt, Jenny and his team are going for the biggest payout possible. And the more he gets now, the better for retirement. "It'll work out."

"I hope so. I don't even know what I want anymore."

I find his neck with my lips. "I know what *I* want."

He laughs, and surprisingly, it sounds easy and free. So damn beautiful. "We need to eat. And I'm pretty sure you have a sound check to get to."

"Eh, fuck 'em. I can be late."

He sits up, shaking his head. "No way. You're not letting your fans down because of me."

"I'd do anything for you." I sit up and kiss him. He indulges me, letting me kiss him softly for a while, but then pushes me back before I can take it any further.

"I know you would, but you're forgetting I'm a fan too, and I don't want to miss this show."

"Fine." We stand up and head out to dinner together.

But we keep our distance the whole time, and it fucking guts me.

RYAN

GRADY WAS worried I'd be bored with the sound check and all the setup before the concert, but he's insane. Watching him sing and play the guitar is one of my favorite things. Always has been. I still remember when we were twelve and he'd pick up his guitar, making up songs and playing classics.

It always made me smile. He's self-taught, something anyone could know from watching his interviews, but no one else actually got to watch the process of him learning.

Except me.

Now, I'm standing backstage next to Waylon watching Grady warm up the crowd. Telling them thank you for being here and how grateful he is to have them all. And I know, without a doubt, it's all genuine.

As long as I can remember, we both wanted out of our small hometown. We both had big dreams of becoming rich and famous, but mostly it was the escape we wanted. Away from small-minded people.

He wanted away from his dad in general, but I wanted a way out of watching my dad struggle. He's a damn good welder and never once complained about providing for his family. Still, over the years, I saw him die slowly inside, watching his beloved game of baseball while his own dreams faded. But then, his faded dreams blossomed into dreams for me.

I love baseball but not like my dad does.

I try not to think about the phone call with my mother and how afraid she sounded at the possibility of me not being re-signed. I try not to let it turn in my gut. The decision between making my dad proud—living his dream of playing for KC—and my own dreams.

Dreams with Grady.

My best friend. The guy I spent all my time with until I was barely eighteen. Who I laughed with and even occasionally shed tears around. The one who knew all my fears and dreams even before I did.

I know deep down what I want, but I don't know if I can face it just yet. I don't know if I can handle disappointing my father, a man who gave everything up for me.

I watch as Grady crosses the stage, not to grab his guitar like I expected, but to sit at a piano in the corner. "What is he doing?" I lean into Waylon.

Waylon just smiles and shrugs. "I don't know. Sometimes he starts the show with a cover."

I watch the band behind him look to Grady for his cue, seemingly not knowing what he's about to play, but it doesn't matter.

From the first note, the recognition hits them, and I feel a tingle run through my body, knowing the song instantly.

"He's not."

"He totally is." Waylon smiles as Grady breaks into a flawless cover of the Queen song, "Love of my Life." And the motherfucker is aiming his thoughtful and heated gaze backstage.

To right where I'm standing.

His fingers glide along the keys as his beautiful voice sings every word, full of emotion and meaning. Directing the lyrics at me. Although the entire crowd probably feels it's being sung to them because he has that ability.

If anyone could see me, we'd be busted in a moment. Because I can't look away. My eyes are locked on him, listening to every single word and note being played. I feel it throughout my entire being.

When the song ends, Grady goes back to the middle of the stage as the crowd erupts, and he grabs his guitar, getting ready for the actual set. I try like hell to regain my wits as I listen to the songs he's written.

About halfway through, I see Waylon texting with someone, then laughing slyly as he puts his phone back in his pocket, and I have to ask, "Someone special?"

"You could say that." He shrugs, but his grin is all sorts of fuckery. "Jenny is pretty damn special."

"Jenny? As in my agent, Jenny?"

He chuckles, watching Grady out on the stage. "That one. She's fierce, but she's pretty damn funny too." He shrugs. "Or maybe she's funny because of how damn fierce she can be."

"It's really weird that you two are friends."

He waves me off, clearly not giving a fuck what I think. "Eh, get over it because she's too good to let go. Can't have enough friends."

I laugh because it's not said with malice, just matter-offactly. "I suppose so. Although I'm not sure Grady and she will ever get along."

"You'd be surprised. Besides she really does have your best interest in mind, and Grady will respect that."

I snort because Jenny is a fantastic agent, but she's looking out for herself, first and foremost. "Yeah, okay."

He turns to me now, his face dripping with honest concern. "We think we can get you exactly what you want, whatever that is."

A cold shiver runs through me as I glance at the stage briefly and then look back to Waylon, unable to voice anything.

But he knows. "Yeah. That."

I don't ask how. I know I have Grady. We're in love and both stubborn motherfuckers. We're going to make this work, no matter what. But how? That's the question. Our careers. Our fathers. Society in general.

Who the fuck knows?

Although Waylon seems to have a pretty good idea.

Instead of asking what Jenny and he have planned or have even been discussing, I ask a different question. "What's it like to be out?"

A slow smile spreads across his face. "Glorious. Freeing." He's still smiling big. "Scary as hell. But oh, so worth it."

I swallow hard, thinking about what it would be like, his answer giving me hope and lighting fire to the dream I've had for a long time.

The concert ends, and before I know it, it's just Waylon, Grady, and me in the dressing room. I'm on a high after watching Grady out there and my talk with Waylon. I want to do something with him. Something fun. Something public.

"Let's go to a bar," I blurt out, gaining instant attention from Waylon and Grady.

Grady steps closer to me, still being careful and not touching me even though we're behind closed doors. "A what?"

"I didn't say a gay bar." I haven't completely lost my damn mind.

Grady shrugs easily. "Hey, I'd do it."

I laugh. "I know you would. But I just meant let's go get a drink. Celebrate a kickass concert."

"Okay." He turns to Waylon. "You coming?"

Waylon tosses his hands up. "Hell, no. I need my beauty rest. But please do me a favor and don't give me any extra PR work, okay? Don't do anything stupid."

"Got it. No public blowjobs." Grady winks at him, and Waylon groans, shaking his head as he leaves.

We use the car service to take us to a nice bar downtown, both of us sitting at the bar and drinking beer. We don't get sloppy drunk or even buzzed, but just hanging out in public is nice. I wish I could grab his hand or lean in and kiss him, but like I said, this is nice.

It's good to catch up and reminisce about growing up together. If anyone heard us talking, it would just seem like two old friends. Not lovers.

Which, of course, makes me slightly bitter.

I try to push it away, excusing myself to go to the bathroom and fighting with myself in the mirror as I wash up after taking care of business. It's good. This is a step. We're out in public together.

So what if I can't touch him the way I want to?

I think about Waylon telling me that eventually, I'll get what I want, being in a bar like this and being able to dance with him and hold his body close to mine. The thought of leaning in for a kiss and not worrying about damaging either of our careers has me taking a deep, relaxing breath and smiling at my reflection in the mirror.

"Someday."

I walk out of the bathroom, which is in the back of the bar and instantly run into Grady. "There you are."

"I wasn't gone that long."

One of his palms flattens against the wall behind me, half-caging me in, and I can feel the heat of his body rolling off him. *God, I love him.* "I was worried."

I quirk an eyebrow. "No, you weren't."

He grins, dragging one hand down my jaw, and when I swallow tightly, his finger trails over the column of my throat, his eyes hungry for me. "We should get out of here."

I nod in agreement, wanting him so goddamn bad. "Yes."

Before I can overthink it, I lean in closer to him, my lips brushing over his in the briefest of kisses. It's only a moment, but I feel it every-fucking-where. "Let's go," he growls as we separate and go back to settle our tab.

We climb into the car and make it back to his hotel, somehow managing not to touch each other. But as soon as we're behind the locked door, our clothes are gone and our mouths are everywhere.

We find ourselves in the bed with a bottle of lube as he gets me ready for him. His fingers probe my hole, scissoring and preparing me for a hungry, desperate fuck we're both dying for.

When I'm flipped over on my stomach, my arms holding me slightly up as he thrusts inside me, hitting deep and connecting our bodies, I feel whole. Every single part of me is filled, and my body thrums with pleasure. My hand reaches between my body and the bed and strokes my cock, chasing my release. I meet each thrust to bring him closer to his own euphoria. I feel only happiness, more content than I've ever been in my life.

This is what I want.

I want him.

GRADY

I'M EXACTLY where I want to be. My head is on Ryan's bare chest as we lay in the hotel bed, both of us totally naked and satisfied from the night before. Going to the bar last night may have been a little reckless, but fuck if I care.

It was fun. Like old times, just us hanging out. Of course, we weren't old enough to actually hang out in a bar back then, but we did have a small tavern that served as a restaurant and a place to play pool. We'd sit with cokes in our hands for hours, talking about nothing. It's some of my best memories.

And last night, we added another one.

But my moment of complete contentedness at waking up next to him goes to shit when I realize what actually woke me up was a loud, repetitive banging on my hotel room door.

"What the fuck?" Ry grumbles, turning over and shoving his face into the pillow, still not a morning person.

"I don't know. I set out the "Do Not Disturb" sign last night."

"Maybe they'll go away," he says, sleep still hanging onto him.

"Open the fucking door." *Oh. Shit.*

Ryan sits up straight now at the sound of his agent's shrill, authoritative voice. "What the hell? How does she even know where I am?"

"You didn't tell her?" I ask, partially amused.

I stand up and pull on a pair of sweats as does Ryan, and he makes his way to the door where Jenny is still pounding away. "Hell, no. I knew she'd freak the fuck out."

"Good plan," I say as he opens the door, and both Jenny and Waylon march inside, closing the door.

Now I know how Jenny found us. I look at Waylon. "Traitor."

He doesn't react. He just holds up his phone. "With good reason. I told you not to give me extra work."

I don't know what he's talking about until my eyes zone in on a blurry, dark picture on his phone. "Oh, fuck."

Ryan grabs it, going pale. "Fuck."

The picture, although low quality, is most definitely from last night. It's of Ryan and me in that hallway outside the bathroom, my arm poised above his hand on the wall and our lips touching.

"Yeah, fuck." Jenny takes the phone, looking at the picture for what I'm sure is the hundredth time and then hands it back to Waylon. "Who do I kill?"

"Me," Ryan says immediately. "It was my idea to go there."

She shakes her head in disappointment, but I don't let her tear into him. "It was definitely my idea to kiss him." I think it was anyway. Really, it was both of us, caught up in the moment.

"Don't." Ryan gives me a firm shake of his head. "I kissed you because I wanted it." He turns back to Jenny. "I fucking wanted it."

His voice is strained, and it actually chips away at my heart, hearing him like that. And damn, it actually makes Jenny, the ice queen, soften ever so slightly. "I know, Ryan."

Waylon gently touches him on the arm. "We just need to sit down and figure out how to get ahead of this."

Ryan shakes his head but sits down on the sofa, followed by me sitting down next to him. Jenny and Waylon take a seat in opposite chairs. "There's no way to, right? I mean, it's out there."

Waylon nods. "It is. I've been tagged so many times overnight. And obviously, my followers are thrilled at the possible coupling."

I smile at that but keep it a small smile. Waylon may have more followers than me on social media. He's a bright light in the LGBTQ+ community, bringing them hope and brightness every fucking day. He's involved in several charities and youth programs. The man is an inspiration, having spent his entire career trying to help the world be a better place.

But his face darkens now. "But that can also turn ugly fast. It's not just on my page. It's everywhere."

"Including in front of the bigwigs we have a meeting with soon," Jenny says solemnly.

"We can fix this," I say even if I'm not completely sure. "I'll say I was fucking around, that I kissed him as a joke."

Ryan winces, and I cringe because it's not a fucking joke, and I know that. "No."

"Ry . . ."

"No," he says firmly. "That will make you look like an ignorant asshole."

"I agree," Waylon says quickly.

I shrug, knowing I'll do anything to help Ry. "So? I'm used to playing that role. It's no big deal. I'll do the dance and apologize for being insensitive and for dragging you into it."

"No," Ryan says yet again, a man of few words.

"Ryan," Jenny sighs, rubbing her temples. "Maybe you should let him do it."

"It's not happening. I'm fucking sick of this."

Jenny, to her credit, isn't yelling and doesn't even seem to be freaking out too badly. Honestly, she just seems tired. "Okay, Ryan. How do you want to handle this? It's a little over a week before our big meeting."

"Maybe I don't give a flying fuck about that meeting anymore. Maybe I'm just done. I'm sick of this." Ryan stands up, his entire body pulling tight with visible tension and anger. "I want to go to a bar with my boyfriend and hold his hand. I want to be able to kiss him in public without anyone batting an eye. I want to fucking love the man I've been in love with for years. Out. Loud."

Jenny doesn't bite back. She doesn't stand up. She stays in her chair with her back straight and a sympathetic look on her face. Waylon looks pained by Ryan's speech, and I'm sure it hurts him deeply.

But it hurts him nowhere as much as it slices me to my core. Because I want that so badly with him. I want to hold him and not worry about where we are when we do what we want to do. I want the freedom to kiss him and say whatever the hell I want to him without thought.

"I want that for you too, Ryan," I say, standing up and walking to where he's standing, grasping his firm shoulders. "But I also want you to have your career."

"Fuck my career."

I've seen him go back and forth on his career, but I've never heard this kind of conviction coming from him about it. "Ryan."

"No." He looks pained. "Maybe I don't want this anymore. If I can't freely be me, who I really am, without having to worry about my contract, maybe I don't want it."

Jenny looks worried but not angry as I turn toward her. "Why don't you guys go grab some coffee or breakfast. We need to talk."

Waylon stands, walking to stand next to her as she rises from her chair, not arguing with me. She looks to Ry. "I'll back you, no matter what you want to do. If it's going to the owners and telling them to fuck off, or if it's coming out and me threatening them within an inch of their lives against any sort of discrimination, I'll do it. You just have to tell me what you want."

Ryan doesn't say anything, but I know he heard her loud and clear. And damn, I'm actually starting to like her.

They leave, and I walk over to Ryan, who's still in a daze. "You can't quit."

"Yes. Actually I can. My contract is up."

"But you aren't done." I grasp his chin to hold his gaze. "You aren't."

"I want you, Grady. Don't you get that? I'm fucking done with this."

I see the anger in his eyes as well as the worn-out expression. "I know you are, but I'm not letting you give up your career for me."

"You say that like you're nothing." He shoves me away, not hard but enough to get space between us.

"Hey, no." I walk him toward the wall until his back hits it.

"You don't get to push me away. You don't get to fucking run because things get hard."

He glares at me. "And you don't get to be nonchalant like none of this fucking matters." He throws my biggest flaw at me without a second thought, and I nod in agreement because I know this isn't something I can brush off. It's not going to just stop being a problem and go away on its own.

I grab the back of his neck, pulling his forehead flush against mine. "Of course, it matters. You're everything to me. You want out of baseball, fine. But if you don't, and I know you don't, then we find a way. You and me, we're a given, not a choice. It's you and me forever, no matter what happens or what is thrown at us. Do you hear me?"

He nods. "I do. I hear you."

"I know you're tired of this shit. I know you're tired of not genuinely being yourself. I hear you. But I know you still love playing. I know you love the sound of the crowd chanting your name and your teammates' names. I know you love the basics—the smell of the leather and the dirt, the fireworks going off above the stadium, the music. I know you love it. And I love you." I tighten my hold on the back of his neck. "We're going to make this happen."

And God help me, we are.

RYAN

I HAVE no idea how Grady thinks we can solve this. It seems damn near impossible. They have a picture of us kissing. But even if there was a small amount of fear when I saw the picture, there was also relief, like I was let out of a cage I've been trapped in for years.

Waylon, Jenny, Grady, and I had lunch delivered to Grady's hotel room, and we're sitting down to eat and discuss. No one is eating.

"Okay, so what do you want to do?"

I look at Jenny after her question and then turn to Grady. We didn't make a plan. But he doesn't answer for me. I turn back to Jenny. "Is it too late to negotiate with LA? With Bennett?"

Her eyebrow arches only slightly, giving away her initial surprise. But before she can say anything, Grady apparently has something to say now. "You want to leave KC?"

The nervous feeling I normally get when thinking about leaving isn't there, not even a little bit. It's what I know. I love and appreciate the fans, but I want to move on. I want it more than I could ever say. "Yes."

He looks stunned by my admission. "You don't have to do this for me. We can work around this."

I shake my head, not wanting to talk it all out right now. I turn to Jenny. "Do you think that would be possible?"

"I think that would be the easiest negotiation I've ever been a part of. You two just won the World Series together. Their team is shit at the moment." Her lips purse like she's carefully considering what she says next. "But are you sure this is what you want?"

"I do." I smile at Grady, hoping to lessen his concern. "I like the idea of being in the same zip code as you again."

That finally lifts his mouth into a fucking grin. "I like that idea too. But we both travel so much, does our zip code really matter?"

"It matters," I confirm quickly. *God, I want this.* I didn't realize how much until now.

Jenny stands, not bothering with her food. "Okay, I'll go make some calls. Try to get it settled before the meeting. If all goes well, you'll be signed with LA before they even get wind of it."

It feels dirty almost to do it that way, but considering they've been fishing around for new talent and have pushed off my negotiations, I'm kind of at the fuck 'em point. "Okay."

"And what about you two?" Jenny asks as she points at me and then drags that finger in Grady's direction.

I answer for him this time because I'm fucking done hiding. "We're together. And once the ink is dried on the contract, we're going out in public together."

"To make a statement?" Jenny doesn't seem against it.

I clear my throat, the prospect of making an official, planned-out statement still making my skin crawl. I look at

Grady. "No." He raises a questionable eyebrow, and I finish my answer, "But I'm not hiding shit. We're going to go out to a restaurant or a bar or whatever the fuck, and if I want to hold his hand, I will. If I want to kiss him, I fucking will."

"But no public statement?" This time it's Waylon with the question.

Grady answers easily, always on the same page, "No, fuck 'em. I didn't have to make a public statement when I started dating Vicky. They all just saw us out in public and assumed."

"But every interview you did after that, they asked about your relationship," Waylon points out.

"So, we'll deal with it then," I say, unbothered because I'm not going on social media and becoming the poster boy for out athletes. *Do I hope this will start a change? Sure. Do I want to be a martyr? No.*

"Yeah. Casually." Grady smiles comfortably. "I like it."

"I fucking love it," I say with my eyes locked on him. And holy shit, it feels good. I know I still need to lay low until I get my contract executed, but this "scandal" is out there. If they sign me already suspecting I'm gay, chances are good they aren't going to give a fuck.

Jenny takes a deep breath, straightening out her skirt and almost looking like a proud mama. "I'm happy for you, Ryan. I really am."

Grady gawks at her, surprise on his face. "Holy fuck, are you crying?"

I examine her face more closely and notice her eyes are indeed glossy. She wipes at her eyes quickly and then raises her middle finger at Grady. "Fuck off. I have PMS, and I have to deal with you assholes."

I grin and stand up, wrapping my arm around her. "That

does sound awful."

Grady leans back in his seat. "Yeah, thank God for having balls and a dick."

She's shooting daggers at him now, and I decide to walk her out before she kills my boyfriend and blames it on momentary hormonal rage. "Thank you, Jenny. Really. I know this hasn't been easy."

A strange look passes over her face, but she doesn't confirm how much of a pain in the ass I am. "This actually makes my life a hell of a lot easier. You know, you're my only client in the middle of the US. All my other ones are on the West Coast."

I did know that. I also know she lives in KC because I've been her most lucrative client so far. "I appreciate it."

"I'll call you when they're ready to sign."

She leaves, and I go back to take a seat with Waylon and Grady, who are both in cheerful moods. Grady laughs, shaking his head. "I can't believe she cried."

Waylon has his phone out and is working as he eats. But he sighs, glancing toward the door Jenny just walked through and then back at Grady and me. "She really cares about you."

Grady and I both share a look, and then Grady snorts. "Yeah. Okay, Waylon."

Waylon, however, doesn't laugh. "You guys, you have to realize how much you mean to her. I think this is a huge weight off her shoulders."

"What do you mean?" I ask as I pop some food in my mouth, my appetite back.

"It was killing her to make you keep that a secret. Trying to put out the fires all the time. Jenny—she's hardcore—but that shit bugged the hell out of her."

I don't think he's wrong about that. Even if she came off

brash nearly all the time, I never got the sense she enjoyed making me hide my sexuality. "Maybe."

"Not maybe. You guys need to give her a break. She's a woman who has a career in a male-dominated field, always having to prove herself." His eyes land on me, but he's not mad. "And you haven't made it easy on her."

"Not his fault he's gay and a baseball player in a world of fucking douchebags."

I laugh. "I'm not arguing about who had it worse. You're right, Waylon."

"We'll send her a gift basket. What do you get for Satan's assistant?" Grady asks, but he's kidding. I know she's grown on him a whole hell of a lot lately.

"Right. Let me handle the gifts." Waylon stands, putting his phone in his pocket. "I'm going to let you two celebrate appropriately and get the hell out of here. Please do Jenny and me a favor . . ." He points his gaze at Grady. "No more trouble for at least a week." He looks at me. "Make it easy on her."

I nod in agreement. Grady salutes him like the asshole he is before Waylon leaves with a sigh, probably assuming they're going to have several fires to put out during the next week despite his warning.

But really, I'm going to do everything I can to make sure this works out.

"Celebrate?" Grady waggles his eyebrows, and I laugh.

"Of course. But after I eat. I think I'm going to need all the energy I can get."

He doesn't argue with that, but he does look troubled, too concerned for his handsome face and normal easy going attitude. "You really want to move away from KC? You know if you want to live in the same zip code, I'll fucking move."

I know he would.

"I need a change. I have to stop living for my parents and the fans. I need to do this for me."

He moves closer to me, his smile over-the-top cheesy. "And that something you need to do . . . That would be me?"

I roll my eyes but lean in and kiss him hard. "You're a dumbass."

He laughs. "So LA, huh?"

"If everything works out."

I shovel food in my mouth, and he leans against the back of the seat. "Well, your music room is kick ass, but mine's better. And so is my pool. I think you'll like it."

I gape at him, my mouth full of food as I try my best to chew and then finally swallow. "Did you just ask me to move in?"

"Why the hell not? Same zip code and you uprooting your life for me? Sounds like this is the logical next step."

I laugh, taking a drink of water to get the food down my throat. "You really do jump head-first into everything."

He looks sheepish. "If you don't want to—"

I stop him by pressing my lips to his—hard. "I want that. I want that so fucking bad. I love that you jump into what you really want. I love that you don't fucking hold back when it counts."

He grins, pressing his lips softly to mine, giving me a reverent kiss and resting his head against mine. "I love that you overthink everything. It's good. I always feel like all our bases are covered."

"We do seem to balance each other out."

He stands up, grabbing my hand and pulling me with him toward the bed. "Fuck the food."

I guess we're celebrating.

FUCK, I don't want to leave him again.

I look over his sleeping form as he hugs his pillow with a muscled arm. The fucker is actually snoring with a little drool at the corner of his mouth, and still, he's the hottest man I've seen.

We've managed to keep a low profile over the past three days, and it turns out Jenny was right. The negotiations with LA have been smooth. They saw the picture of Grady and me, but, according to Jenny, they didn't even bat an eye. Which bodes well for the future, I suppose. But I don't care if they can handle it or not. If they give me a contract with a loophole in case things get too hot, they can buy my ass out and I'll be Grady's tour bitch.

I love playing baseball. I do. But if baseball can't love me back for who I am, then we need to break up.

However, at the moment, there seems to be a glaringly bright possibility that I'll be playing for a while. Jenny thinks they'll be able to sign us by the end of the week. Which means I'm on a plane back to KC tonight, where Bennett is, so we can meet with them together. Apparently, they're all set to meet us at our lawyer's office.

It'll all be worth it soon enough. Will the fans be pissed? Yeah, for sure. Will my parents fucking lose it? Yeah, probably.

But I can't keep living like this. It's never been worth it before, but as soon as Grady came back into my life and there was hope I'd get to be with him, everything changed for me. All of this will be 100 percent worth it if I can just finally have him.

"Hey." I look over to see Grady's eyes cracked open and peering at me. "You're thinking too hard."

I grin and move closer to his body, reaching under the sheet and stroking his already stirring cock. "Hard, you say? Not quite."

He laughs. "Now who's the corny one?"

I kiss him, not caring about morning breath or anything else because, goddamn it, it's my last day with him and I need him. And he doesn't seem to mind either when he grasps my hair and shoves his tongue in my mouth.

"Show me how much you're going to miss me."

I do just that, stroking his now fully erect shaft, paying special attention to the sensitive tip and making his hips involuntarily thrust upward. "Like this?"

"That's good." He tips his head back, exposing his throat to me. I take full advantage, sliding my mouth over his skin that's pulled tight with erotic tension.

"I really am going to miss you." He grabs my ass with both hands, tugging my full weight onto him and forcing me to straddle him, gripping my ass cheeks and not letting go.

"I'm going to miss you too." His hands slide over the planes of my back as I look down at his cock, continuing to stroke him after grabbing the lube and making sure he's nice and slick. He steals some lube from his cock and moves one hand to my aching dick, stroking me. I was already hard, but when his hand grips me, I nearly lose it, going from hard to *achingly* hard.

"Fuck, Grady."

"We can do that, but right now," he says, thrusting into my hand, and I do the same with his, "I'm too fucking close."

"Me too."

I lean down enough to kiss him while we jerk each other off, chasing our mutual pleasure. My body strains with tension, craving the release his hand promises. The room is quiet except for our moans and heavy breathing. It's not long before we're both spilling over each other's hands and making a sticky mess that neither of us give two fucks about.

I lay next to him, my head on his heart and think about what a future with him will look like.

I'm not really sure about the details and realize there will, no doubt, be challenges.

But, at the end of the day, it's going to be fucking beautiful.

GRADY

I'M on my usual high after a concert, but it's coupled with nerves when I walk into the dressing room backstage and immediately look around for my phone. Ryan's meeting with the LA baseball team was today.

It was hours ago, but with the fucking time difference and sound checks, I haven't had a chance to talk to him yet. My mind has been on him all day. My body and mind have been strung out with nervous energy, needing to know the next move.

I was completely serious when I asked him to move in with me. I want it to happen. And at this point, if he isn't moving to LA, I'm moving back to Kansas City. I don't really give a fuck where my address is as long as it's the same as Ryan's.

The idea of sharing a roof with him is all-consuming for me now. It's all I think about. And I want it.

I find my phone and see a text from him, telling me to give him a call when I can. Apparently, I'm dick-whipped because I immediately call him. And he must be equally whipped because he answers right away. I'm graced with his beautiful face and his tired, but happy, eyes. "Hey, finally found time for me, huh, rockstar?"

I laugh and settle into the sofa in the dressing room. "And what about you? Are you a former professional baseball player or still a current one?"

He's sitting in bed, shirtless with disheveled hair, and if I had to guess, I'd say he'd been asleep before I called. "Current."

I don't bother hiding the grin that's so wide it feels like my cheeks are going to split. "Contract?"

"Signed. With Bennett."

Relief washes over me. "How many years?"

"Three." God, he looks happy. "And twice what KC was struggling to pay. I'm set."

"Good. And the fans?"

His muscles pull tight as he shrugs and looks adorably guilty, yet still sure of his decision. "They'll be pissed we're leaving. I'm okay with it though. I've paid my dues."

"You've committed no crime." I have to throw in some "Bohemian Rhapsody" lyrics.

He rolls his eyes. "Always about Queen with you, huh? Why don't you stick to your own lyrics?"

I laugh. "Don't you know it's impossible to write a good song when you're happy, Bailey?"

"I've really fucked you over, huh?"

"You really did. You owe me."

"Want me to break your heart?"

"Hell, no." I don't even hesitate. "You're never getting away from me now."

"Sounds stalkery."

I chuckle. "I'll find you."

He shakes his head, raising one arm in the air to yawn, and I sit back to bask in the arm porn. If I sensed any hesitance at all in him, I'd question him about wanting to move, but I only see happiness and relief on his handsome face. "So, when are you coming to me?"

He laughs, and God, I've missed that sound. How the hell did I go seven years without that sound? "I don't have to be at spring training until the middle of February. So, I'm yours until then."

"You're fucking mine always. When do you move in?"

Again, with the fucking gorgeous laughter. "Whenever you're ready for me. You seem pretty busy though."

I run my fingers through my hair, content. More content than I've ever been in my life. The love of my life is happy with his career and is moving in with me. "You want me to cancel this fucking tour right now?" Waylon walks inside my room, not even slightly bothered by our conversation as he takes a seat next to me. "I'll do it."

"Oh, he will," Waylon says dramatically, waving at Ry. "Hey Ryan. How did it go?"

He walked into only the last part of our conversation, and even though he walked in when I offered to cancel my tour, he seems happy. My guess is he already talked to Jen-nay.

Ryan sits up further in the bed, and I get lost in the view of his chiseled pecs for a moment before he answers, "No. I don't want you to cancel, dumbass. I'm coming to you. We'll figure out the whole moving thing whenever."

"Actually, I'm coming to you in two days."

"Is that so?"

Waylon confirms, having no problem butting into our conversation like the brother I never wanted but am glad I now have. "Yup. Kansas City. Three nights."

Ryan's eyes do a happy celebration while the rest of him remains cool and collected. "Well, alright then. I'll leave the light on for you, Grady."

"You fucking better, Bailey. I'm so fucking proud of you."

And I mean it. None of this is easy. He doesn't want to hide anymore, and I get that. But it doesn't mean any of this is going to be easy, regardless of his new team seemingly being cool with it.

The world still has a ways to go.

"Love you."

"Love you."

"I love you both," Waylon sings, and we all laugh before I hang up with Ryan.

He's moving in with me in LA. We're going to share not only a zip code but an address, and I finally feel whole.

After seven years of trying to figure out the source of this emptiness inside me, despite having what the world would say was everything, I found the missing piece.

And I'm not letting him go.

RYAN

"I CAN'T BELIEVE you're really doing this, Ryan. How can you leave your fans behind? Your home?"

"Mom, they didn't want to pay for me to stay. It's a business decision."

My mother waves me off, extremely irate on the dreaded video call I knew I'd receive. The news broke pretty damn fast that Bennett and I are done with Kansas City and will start the new season out on the West Coast. So I knew it was only a matter of time before I received the call from my parents.

And yet, I don't feel as ashamed as I thought I would. I don't feel the need to explain much to them. I'm twenty-five years old. I've been on my own for years, and I just signed a major, record-breaking contract.

Not to mention, I have the man of my dreams in the master bathroom who's singing in the shower at the moment. He flew in yesterday for the first night of his Kansas City engagement, and after the concert, we came back to my house and spent our time catching up. In bed.

We even managed to talk a little.

My father is sitting next to my mom, but he hasn't said

much. I knew he wouldn't be happy with this news. "You need to have some loyalty, Ryan. Is this about your dating life?"

I wince. She did not just imply that I want to go to LA because I'm gay. "I'm happy, Mom. And I'm already dating someone from here."

She looks slightly pale and opens her mouth to say something but then doesn't. Good. I don't want to hear her lecture me about how I haven't found the right woman. "You're leaving home."

"I left home seven years ago."

She waves me off. "You know what I mean. You're killing your father."

I look at my dad, who's stayed quiet throughout the entire conversation. "Then he can tell me that himself, but still . . ." I lessen the bite in my tone. "It wouldn't change anything. I'm happy. For the first time in a long time, I'm happy. I have everything I want."

I hear the shower turn off and Grady saunters in with a towel around his waist, walking to his duffle bag across the room.

"I gotta go. Love you guys."

I barely let them say their goodbyes before I hang up and walk to Grady, untying the knot around his waist as he finds his jeans, picking them up. "You okay?"

I nod absently, my front against his back, and kiss the top of his spine. His skin is warm and still moist from the shower. "My parents are having a hard time with my move."

I pull the towel away and let my fingers slide over his taut abs. "And are you?"

"Oh, I'm hard." I press my growing erection against his naked ass. I'm in sweats, but not for long.

He chuckles and turns to face me. "You really okay?"

"You having second thoughts?"

He shakes his head immediately, never letting any doubt creep in. "Never." His fingers move through my hair. "I'm so fucking sorry, Ry."

I'm taken aback, my heart speeding up while I try to figure out what he's talking about. "About what?"

"I should have come after you years ago."

I wave him off, moving back to my bed and sitting on the edge. "I'm sorry I ran."

"I could have found you." I guess we aren't playing at the moment. He tugs his jeans on, sans briefs, and sits down next to me. "I should have found you. Instead, I let us walk around numbly for seven years without each other." He waves his arms around my bedroom. "We could have had this for seven years."

I shake my head. "Don't do that."

"Do what?"

"The what-ifs. They'll fucking kill us. I was a chickenshit and ran. You were a chickenshit and let me stay gone. But maybe we wouldn't have all this . . ." I mimic his previous gesture, "if we hadn't done that."

"I'm still sorry."

"Fine." I pull him to me, my hand on the back of his neck. "We're both sorry motherfuckers. But I love you. And all that matters now is that I'm never letting you go."

"Good." He kisses me.

"Let's go get some coffee."

His eyebrow arches. "Coffee?"

"Yup. It's fucking cold outside, but the coffee is worth it."

He stands up, finding a shirt and tugging it on while I grab my tennis shoes. "You think Justin will be there?"

I roll my eyes as we walk downstairs to grab our coats. "Be nice."

He doesn't agree, of course, and when we arrive at the coffee shop, mischief is written all over his beautiful face. This was probably a bad idea. And not because I'm worried about the photographers that are somehow already here when we walk inside.

No, it's because for a moment, I forgot that Grady is one seriously jealous man. Not gonna lie, I don't hate it. We walk up to the counter, and his eyes are locked on me just as Justin approaches with a happy grin. "Ryan Bailey! You're here." Pouting playfully, he adds, "But I heard you're leaving us."

Grady wraps an arm around my waist and pulls me to him tightly. I know if I shoved him away right now, he wouldn't say anything, but I don't do that. Instead, I lean in. "I am."

Justin's eyes track our close proximity, but he says nothing. "Your usual?" I nod, and he looks to Grady. "And what can I get you?"

"Well," he drawls. *Oh boy.* "You know I recently tried new things and found I love it. So, I'll take that sugary drink you made last time. Nothing wrong with experimenting, Justin. But there's nothing wrong with sticking to what you love either."

A smile plays on my lips as well as Justin's as he nods and gets to work. I lean into Grady's ear. "You're an idiot."

"I'm your idiot." He doesn't whisper it, and I don't tense up at the possibility of anyone hearing.

Rumors are going to spread fast, and most of them will be true.

But not one part of me can find it in myself to give a fuck.

He's my idiot alright.

GRADY

"Mr. Bell, one question please!" I look over at the kid outside the arena in downtown Denver and take pity on him. He looks fresh out of college—maybe. Hell, he may still be in school and probably dying to get an exclusive interview.

Luckily, I have Waylon right here with me in case I get in a jam. Not that Ryan and I have been shy about our relationship.

He went on tour with me for a month before he had to report to training camp last week, and we didn't bother to hide a goddamn thing.

Waylon gives me a quick nod of permission, and I approach the kid instead of going inside. "No problem, but I needed to be at sound check ten minutes ago."

The guy, who's small in stature and honestly kind of cute with his wide eyes behind thick black-framed glasses, grabs his iPhone excitedly. "Okay. Thank you. I'll only be a minute. This is for my followers. And I know they love you just as much as I do. Well, maybe."

He grins, and I laugh. "Sounds good."

He quickly pulls up an Instagram Live feed and does an

amazingly fast introduction where I don't catch every word but can't help smiling at his enthusiasm.

"Okay, so like I said, I have Grady Bell here, outside the arena." He points the camera at me. "I'm assuming you're here for the concert tonight."

I beam into the camera, putting on my best show, preferring these impromptu interviews far more than the scheduled ones I typically avoid. "I suppose that's why I'm here. I hear the band is pretty good."

The kid laughs, but I can tell it's real and not forced for his followers on Insta. "So, we won't keep you long, but I just wanted to say you're a true inspiration. Singing songs that really speak to the heart and then following your heart. Doing what you want."

He doesn't specifically say anything about my relationship with Ryan, and fuck if I don't want to stake my claim on him right now, where I know it'll eventually be shared all over. But I can't just yet. I want Ry to get settled into his new role in LA first.

"I appreciate that. Music has a way of saying things we can't always get out when we're just talking."

"Oh, I agree. Your music saved me. I talk about it all the time."

I wonder what exactly that means and pause, seeing the tear sliding down his cheek as he wipes it away. I pull him into a quick side hug. "I'm happy to hear that. You're a good person. You deserve all good things. I can feel it."

He smiles brightly, standing a little taller, and I know the kid isn't here for a hard-hitting interview. He's actually a fan.

"I'm really sorry, but I actually am late."

"No problem. I just wanted to say that and to ask if you're going to do another tour next year. We need your music."

I turn to Waylon, who doesn't offer an answer. I've pretty much already told him I'm taking time off after this tour, but it's not public knowledge yet. And I know it will be a headache for Waylon if it is. "You know I never say never." I wink at the camera, and the kid laughs.

"Not exactly an answer, but we'll take it. Thanks so much, Grady Bell!"

I laugh at the use of my whole name, and we say a quick goodbye to his followers before he logs off and then shakes my hand excitedly. "Thank you, thank you, thank you! I've been a huge fan for so long, and I wasn't bullshitting when I said you saved me."

"Thank you for not bringing up certain things." I'm careful, but he knows what I mean.

He shrugs. "I'm never going to out anyone. That's a shitty move. I mean, I pretty much came out as soon as I was out of the womb, but it doesn't matter. Until you're ready to share that —if you ever are—it's no one's business."

I wink at him and start toward the door, but then turn toward him. "Hey, kid. What's your name?"

"Dawson." He cringes. "My mom was a big fan of that *Creek* show."

I laugh at that. "Okay, um." I can't shake my smile. "When we're ready, I'd love to give you the exclusive."

"Really?" He brightens up.

I nod toward Waylon. "Can you get his info?"

Waylon is already at his side. "On it. Now, go."

I laugh because he's a manager first. "Thanks." I turn to Dawson. "We'll talk soon."

He's giddy, and I'm grinning from ear-to-ear as I walk into sound check.

We aren't totally out yet, but it's coming, and I have a good feeling about this kid.

Hopefully, Ry will be on the same page. Though I think we'll wait till he's done with baseball if that's the way he wants it. Neither of us is interested in making a great big gay statement. No one has to come out and say they're straight, so fuck 'em.

But I do have a good feeling about the kid.

Still, we're going to do it our way and at our time.

RYAN

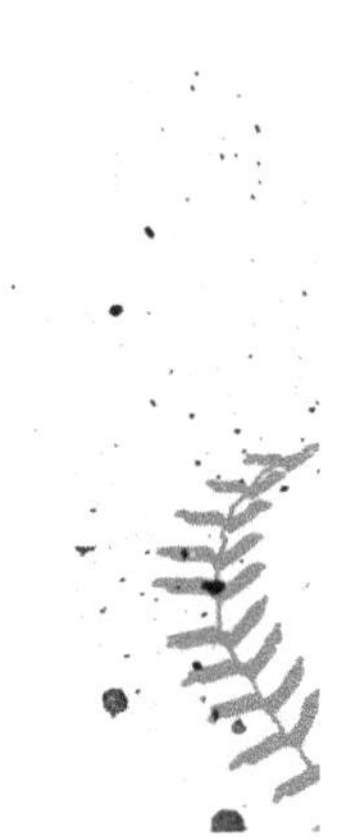

I sit on the bench in the locker room as Bennett ties the laces on his cleats. *Most of the* guys have filtered out of the locker room already, and I try like hell not to let my nerves get to me. Most of my new teammates seem to have accepted Bennet and me with open arms, but I'm still wary.

It feels like the first day of school. We both know we have something to prove tonight. Prove to the fans and the team we're worth every penny.

But still, Bennett and I are fucking solid. Training went smoothly, and we're ready for this shit.

"Okay, I have to ask you . . ." I look over at Bennett expectantly. "The rumors?"

I almost laugh but don't. He hasn't asked me all spring. But now he's going to? Okay. "What rumors?"

He shoves my shoulder. "Don't be an asshole. Are they true?"

He doesn't look disgusted or even nervous about my answer. He already knows but wants it confirmed. It's the worst-kept secret nowadays.

Grady and I don't hide. We go where we want when we want, but still we've avoided any actual straight-forward questions, and we haven't put out a statement. It isn't our style, and honestly, it isn't going to happen.

At least not a professionally worded, well thought-out Tweet.

"I'm gay."

He nods, standing up and walking toward the door. "Okay, then."

"What the fuck?" I stand up, smiling and walk to him. "That's it? No questions?"

"What, like who's the pitcher and who's the catcher?"

I roll my eyes and shove him. He laughs. "No, asshole."

"You really want to talk about assholes?" He cocks his head to the side, and I grab the handle to the door.

"Nevermind. You really are a shithead."

He stops me from leaving. "You're the shithead. You could have told me. It's not like I didn't suspect . . . maybe."

Not surprised. "You never said anything."

He shrugs. "It's not like it mattered, but you could have told me."

I do feel shitty for keeping it a secret all this time. "I'm sorry. I didn't want to put that burden on you. Keeping a secret like that doesn't feel good for anyone."

"I'm sorry you had to." He raises an eyebrow. "But not anymore?"

I shake my head. "Nah, it's nobody's business who I fuck . . ."

"That being Grady Bell."

"Who knew you were such a fucking gossip queen?"

He laughs, pulling the door open so we can walk out. The game is starting soon. "No more secrets, dickhead. I mean it. I'm happy for you, even if my wife is pretty damn disappointed Grady is off the market."

"Did you hear what you just said? She's your wife."

He laughs easily, shrugging it off with confidence and playfulness. "Eh, I know I'm her second choice. I've dealt with it, Ry."

I laugh at his joke because that woman is head over heels for him, crush on my man or not. "Still, I hope we'll still get invites to your famous cookouts."

He nudges my shoulder. "Of course, you will. Just gotta keep an eye on our significant others."

I can hear the crowd already as we walk out to the field. God, I love that sound. Not quite as much as Grady singing or his laugh . . . but it's right up there with my favorite sounds.

"Let's go show these motherfuckers how we do it," I say as we jog out to warm up.

Who knew I could have everything I want? Not me. But I'll fucking take it.

GRADY

IT'S the last concert of this tour and my last one for a while, although not many people know that yet. Ryan tried to fight with me about it, but I'm taking a couple of years off. I'm more than okay with that. It'll give me time to write new songs and just be with him.

This way, when I want to, I can travel with him.

I'm happy. Holy fuck, am I happy. It's the best time of my life, and I'm not going to squander it.

I stroke the dark black facial hair I've grown out on tour. I'm not sure whether I'm going to keep it, but Ry doesn't seem to mind, so maybe I will. I try to ignore the slight tremor in my hand as I address the crowd from my position at center stage. "Well hello, Los Angeles! Man, it's good to be home!"

The crowd shouts happily. I do consider this my home, despite being from Kansas. It's where I've begun to build my life with Ryan. It's where our house is, where we'll live together when we aren't traveling. And until we both officially retire and buy that private island somewhere—yeah, I doubt it will happen, but never say never—this is our home.

The baseball team here has more than embraced Ryan, and

we still don't hide when we go out in public. Our secret is a poorly kept one, and the city seems to be okay with it.

And for the record—if they weren't, it wouldn't matter. I haven't felt this free or this happy in a really long time, and nothing will ruin it. Nothing.

"As you all know, this is my last show for a while." I'm met with the normal boos as expected, but when I look backstage and see Ry's wicked smile, I can't help but match his energy as I look out at the crowd. "I know, I know. But you guys want more songs, right?" Cheering. But it's woeful. "Okay. So I can guarantee you tonight will be the best damn show you've ever seen!"

The crowd roars, and I look over at Ryan, who's standing next to Waylon and Dawson. Dawson has been a frequent visitor at our house, along with Waylon, who assures me there's nothing going on, that he's just taken the kid under his wing. I don't push because, honestly, I'm not sure if anything *is* going on.

All I know is I made sure Dawson was here tonight and that he was live-streaming the beginning of this concert.

Because it's going to be something to see.

Okay, Bell, you can do this. Don't be a pussy. "So, some of you may or may not know that I've been seen around town a hell of a lot with a special person. My best friend." Ry cocks his head to the side as I look at him but keep my body toward the crowd. "Now, I'm not going to embarrass him and make him come out here with me." I face the crowd now, smiling. "But I want everyone to know just how much he means to me."

The crowd goes wild, and I mean, they're losing their shit. When I turn to see what has them so riled up, I see Ryan approaching me, walking with that strong, confident glide in my direction until he stops only a foot from me, stealing my mic. "I don't embarrass easily."

I laugh because that's true. Ry is stone-cold most of the time. People can't read him. I take the microphone back. "Ah, true. But I bet I could make you blush."

He gives me a *don't you dare* look, and I laugh. The crowd hoots and hollers as my heart punches rapidly in my chest.

"So, the thing about my best friend, the man I've known nearly my entire life is that he loves hard. Fiercely. *Particularly.* First baseball . . ." I grin at him. "And then me."

He rolls his eyes, leaning into the mic. "I think that's the wrong order."

And again, the crowd loses it. And it's a big, big audience, so it's loud. "The thing about me is—I sing about love and how it tears you apart. I wasn't sure I believed in it because I saw too much hate, but Ry, he makes me believe. In everything."

A collective "aw" comes from the crowd. Then I drop to one knee, and I think my eardrums might explode from the roar of the crowd, but all I can do is look up at Ry as I take his hand in mine. "I know we said no big announcements. No Tweets."

"Right." Ry wants to be mad. I can see it, but I can also see he's not, not even a little. He looks almost childlike with that grin on his face. "But a crowded arena with our friend Dawson live-streaming?"

"Go big or go home, right, Bailey?"

He chuckles, "Get on with it."

"Marry me." Not a question. It's a demand because it's the only thing that makes sense."

"Yes. I'll marry you." Yeah, I think my ears are bleeding. I didn't think this through because I've never heard a crowd so frenzied as when he raises me up to him and pulls me in for a kiss. "I love you, you fucking asshole."

"You love my asshole?" He rolls my eyes and covers the mic with his hand. "I love you too."

When he releases me, we still hug our bodies close. I look over at Dawson, who's tearing up as he tells the world that Ryan Bailey is mine.

Officially.

RYAN

After that kind of proposal, who wouldn't be on a high? After the concert, we came home, fucked, talked for a bit, had champagne, fucked again, and then passed out. And now, we're in our bed the next morning, and I can't stop smiling.

An affliction I'm not used to but I like. "So, when do you want to do this?"

"I'm thinking right after you win the World Series for the second time."

I laugh because the team has improved, but we aren't going to the World Series this year. Maybe next year though. "Or after the regular season ends."

He pulls me in for a kiss. "Or right fucking now. I can't wait."

I laugh against his lips. "Always 100 percent all-in, aren't you?"

"When it comes to you, yeah."

I know. I groan when my phone rings because the only person I want to talk to is right here, but then I groan again when I see it's a video call from my mom. "Ugh. No."

"We have to face them sometime. I'm sure the news is out everywhere."

"I figured it would be Jenny."

He laughs at that like it's the funniest thing he's ever heard. "Are you fucking kidding me? I asked her for your hand in marriage before I got down on one knee. I don't have a death wish."

My eyes widen. "You asked Jenny?"

"Of course, I did."

I can't hold back the bark of laughter and shake my head. "She has you trained."

"That makes two of us." I don't argue because she's helped so damn much with the new contract and fielding questions we weren't ready to answer yet. I'm glad he let her know.

He hits answer on my phone, and I glare at him before my mom's face pops up on my phone. I see my dad right next to her. "Ryan." She sounds distraught. Just fucking great.

"Hey, Mom."

Her eyes dart next to me to where Grady is sitting. We're both bare chested, and there's no hiding the fact that we're in bed together, not that I would.

"Grady." She sounds breathless. "Is it true?"

"Yes, ma'am. I'm sorry I didn't get a chance to ask for Ry's hand."

"This isn't a joke," my mother cuts him off quickly, starting to cry, and I recoil, already wanting to hang up. I love my parents. I do. I'm grateful for all the things they sacrificed for me, but I don't want anything tarnishing my happiness with Grady.

"No, it's not. I love Ryan. Nothing about this is a joke. We're getting married."

She gapes at Grady. "But you're straight."

Grady laughs easily, taking the phone casually from my shaking hand. "Apparently I'm not."

How can he say that so easily? It took me so fucking long to tell these people I was gay, and they just swept it away like it wasn't real. And I let them do that for so long. "Your father—"

Grady cuts her off quickly, "Has no role in my life. He's been blowing up my phone for weeks, so I've changed my number. I want nothing to do with him."

"But Grady—"

Again, he doesn't let her speak, but his tone softens, "Look, I know you love your son, but you need to love all of him. Or you're going to miss out on a whole hell of a lot. Our wedding. Our kids."

"Kids?" I raise my eyebrow playfully. That's not something we've talked about.

"Opposed?"

"No," I answer quickly because I think we'd both make amazing fathers, and all of a sudden, I want that with him badly.

"Well, I suppose that's not as bad as you playing for LA." Grady and I both turn our attention to my father, and my jaw drops at his first words.

"What?"

He shrugs his shoulder uncomfortably. "I'm proud of you, Ryan. I just want you to be happy. Even if it's in LA."

He says LA with disgust, but it's playful. The whole sentence sounded genuine. "Really?"

He looks directly into the camera. "Yes, really. You've always made me proud. Always working to achieve the highest goals, and now you're in love. There's nothing wrong with that."

My mother gasps, "But—"

My dad cuts her off this time, "But nothing. You know you love weddings, and you want grandchildren. No need to ruin that chance."

My mother wipes at her face, and she breathes deeply. "I do love you, Ryan."

"I love you too." It's true, even if we don't see eye-to-eye on much and I wish she wasn't so damn closed-minded.

"And we love Grady."

"Good," I say firmly. "That's nonnegotiable."

"What about LA? Is that up for negotiation?" my dad jokes, and I shake my head.

"I don't think so, Dad."

"Well," he says, scratching his chin. "I don't think I can stomach going there to watch a home game, but when you come here, you can bet I'll be in the crowd."

"I'll get you VIP seats."

They both wave me off, and we talk for a while longer before we say our goodbyes. I put my phone on the table next to me and lean against Grady. "Did that really just happen?"

He chuckles, his shoulder moving with the movement. "I think your dad is more pissed about you playing for LA than you being gay with me."

"Gay with you?" I look up at him, amused.

"You better not be gay with anyone else."

I roll my eyes. "You're fucking ridiculous."

"I know, but you love me." I kiss him softly, letting my hand rake down his toned abs. "I do. Want me to show you how much?"

"Yes, please."

I'm glad my parents seem to be coming around, but even if they weren't, it wouldn't matter.

Nothing else matters but this.

GRADY

Almost Three Years Later

"Ladies and gentlemen, we're here. We're witnessing the last play of Ryan Bailey's career. And what a career it's been." I can hear the announcer, but my eyes are on my husband.

He could have signed another contract. Hell, he could have negotiated a huge contract, considering his team is about to win his third World Series, but he doesn't want it.

I've been taking time off the past three years, being a baseball husband and enjoying the holy hell out of it. Doesn't hurt that my husband's ass looks fucking great in those baseball pants, but still.

I don't follow him every time he travels, but more often than not, I do. Especially if I can fit in an interview in the city he's in, keeping the band relevant. My record label actually has been pretty damn cool about the whole thing. I either misjudged them, or they just didn't want to deal with a scandal. Or maybe Jenny got to them.

Who knows?

I've still been writing songs and keeping up with Immoral. And maybe after some much-needed time of both of us being off work, I might go back on tour.

"And that's it, folks!" I smile as the game ends and Ry's team rushes the field in another victory. "Ryan Bailey, the city of LA thanks you," the announcer says warmly, and I wait for my man on the sidelines, ready to start our new life.

As Ryan remains busy with reporter after reporter, I decide to finally check my phone, and my heart speeds up in a panic.

Oh, fuck.

I see missed phone calls from Jenny and Waylon as well as several texts from both of them.

"Fuck." I try to call Waylon, but there's no answer.

Ry's eyes meet mine through the crowd. He must sense my panic because he makes his way to me. "What's wrong?"

Before I can answer a large microphone is shoved in my face. "Grady Bell, how proud are you of your husband?"

"Grady Bailey, actually." Ry was more than willing to hyphenate our names, but I wasn't having it. I don't want anything to do with my father's last name, and I'm happy as hell to have Ryan's.

"Right." The reporter looks slightly flustered but quickly rebounds, "Well, how happy are you for your husband, Mr. Bailey?"

"Super proud. Always."

"Can you please give us a minute?" Ry asks politely, and thankfully, the reporter and his crew get the hint. He immediately turns to me. "What's wrong?"

"I have a shitload of missed calls from Waylon and Jenny."

"Fuck."

"I know."

Finally, my phone rings in my hand, and I answer when I see it's Waylon, "What's going on?"

"Jesus. Now you finally answer your phone!" I hear Waylon's frantic tone, and a bucket of ice water may as well have been poured over my head because I'm freaked the fuck out.

"I'm sorry, we were a little busy. What's going on?"

"Jenny's in the hospital. Get here now."

"Shit."

Ryan and I don't waste any time and get out of there. Waylon is a miracle worker and gets us immediately on a chartered jet from Colorado back to California. After what feels like an eternity but, in reality, is only a short time, we arrive at the hospital.

We're greeted by a weary Waylon, who looks worn the fuck out. "Finally."

"Where is she?" Ryan asks, and Waylon leads us into the hospital room where Jenny is lying in a bed. But she's not alone. Not anymore.

"Oh my God." The gasp comes from me as I see the bundle in her arms. "Jen-nay."

She looks beautiful with her black hair tied up and no makeup on, but she's smiling even through the glare she directs my way. "I gave birth to your kid, and you still use that stupid nickname?"

"He's sorry." Ry has tears in his eyes as he approaches the bed. "She's here. Already?"

"Yeah. I thought we had two more weeks." The sweet girl wraps her pinky around Jenny's finger and looks up at Ry with her big blue eyes. It's like she knows she belongs to him.

But she's my girl too.

We both put sperm in the equation, and who knows whose actually won out. We don't care. As far as we're concerned, little Kristy is both of ours. And thank God for our friend, Jenny, who deserves one hell of a raise for this.

"You okay?" Ryan asks her, placing a hand on our baby's head.

"I'm fine. Really. They gave me an epidural quickly, and I didn't feel shit."

"I was there for that gore-fest, though, and I'd appreciate a raise," Waylon says from his seat next to the bed.

Ryan and I both chuckle as Jenny situates herself in the bed and smiles at Ryan. "Since you're my favorite, you take her first."

Ry doesn't argue. When he lifts our girl into his arms, I realize I thought I was whole before, but that was only one chapter of our story because now everything is right in the world. Nothing can touch me.

The love of my life is holding the love of our lives, and that's it for me. I'm fucking done.

"Wow." I can't say anything more than that, and when Ryan moves to my side and places Kristy in my arms, I take a moment to deeply breathe in her sweet scent, taking in every detail from her tiny nose, big eyes, and tiny little hands. "She's perfect."

Ryan is beaming. "She is. She's everything, Grady."

"She's a Bailey." I grin.

He takes my hand as I hold our girl, surrounded by our best friends.

Maybe I should have immediately followed Ry all those years ago. Maybe he shouldn't have left, but it doesn't matter. Maybe I should have had the courage to tell him how I felt even if I didn't really understand it back then. I kissed him because I loved him. I know that now. But none of it matters.

None of it.
Because I have him.
And we have her.

RYAN

THINGS AREN'T 100 percent perfect. I mean, are they ever?

But they're as close to perfect as I can imagine. Kristy is a perfect, happy baby. But she has her own personality, and she fusses, letting us know when she isn't pleased with her dads. And yeah—she's going to be spoiled as hell, but we don't care.

"Fuck. I'll get her," Grady grumbles from his side of the bed, but I laugh him off.

"I'll get her. It was your turn last time."

It's the middle of the day anyway, and we were trying to do what they say and nap when the baby is napping.

"Nah, you got her three times before that."

He climbs out of bed, wearing only a pair of gray joggers that hug his ass perfectly and still turn me the fuck on even sleep-deprived and after nearly four years together.

There's nothing he can do to turn me off.

But when he holds our two-month-old baby to his bare chest, bouncing her and soothing her?

Yeah. Nothing fucking hotter in this universe.

I don't miss baseball as much as I thought I would. I figure in a few years, if I do miss it, maybe I'll go into sports broadcasting or something sports-related. But I wouldn't mind having a few more Kristys either. Of course, I'm pretty sure Jenny is out.

She loves being Aunt Jenny, but she told me, and I quote, "I'm not pushing anything else out of my vagina." After that horrible image, Waylon, Grady, and I decided we were okay with that.

We can get another surrogate who won't talk about all the gory details.

But we love Jenny. She's not only my manager but has become one of our best friends, and we can never repay her for giving us Kristy.

"I think she's hungry," Grady says, laying her in my arms as he goes to heat a bottle.

I smile when I see a text from my mom, telling me they got their flight confirmation. I text her back, telling her we can't wait and send her a quick baby pic to tide her over.

Kristy sucks on my finger as she waits somewhat patiently for Grady to get back. When he does, he takes her and moves to the rocking chair in the corner to feed our girl.

"Mom and Dad will be here next Wednesday."

"Good." He smiles, and it's real. My parents attended our wedding and now seem to be pretty damn open and supportive of our marriage. My mom especially is excited about her beautiful granddaughter and never lectures us. She refers to Grady as my husband, as she should, and for now, all is right in the world.

Grady's father has openly spewed hatred toward us, but we just ignore and block him. Because no one deserves that kind of toxicity in their lives. That's what the block button is for, and yeah, you can use it in real-life.

No love lost there.

And thankfully, we have more than enough love in this house to make up for it. Our kids are going to grow up in a house full of love and acceptance where nothing else is tolerated.

And it's a beautiful thing.

The End

NOTE FROM THE AUTHOR

I want to thank you for reading Ryan and Grady's story. Man, I love them. They were so hard to let go! I really didn't want it to end because their love is beautiful to me.

I want to live in a world full of acceptance, where love is never hated and no one has to hide. I hope you enjoyed their story.

I know some of it may seem exaggerated, and admittedly, I don't know a lot about the inner workings of the sports/rockstar world, but it is fiction after all. And this sort of stuff does happen. No one should have to live in fear, whether perceived or real. Everyone should be free to love who they love.

I love MM romance, but I wasn't sure I could write it properly. Hopefully I did them justice because Ryan and Grady will remain in my heart forever.

I want to thank Elle, Ari, and Emma for telling me I could do this and supporting me the entire time, even when I was a super cranky bitch and had to put myself in timeout. I love you all! But don't be gross.

Thank you, Jeanna, for always being your most amazing self. And thanks to all my friends who have always been there for me. I want to thank my family for their love and support, especially my poor husband who had to deal with my cranky self in person.

I had this idea for a summer of standalones—four books in four months, and I'm the first one to tell you, I'm totally insane. I have two kids under seven and am a wife, daughter, sister, friend, and a total freaking nut.

But I'm almost there now!

I hope you've enjoyed this book and will consider leaving a review! Love you all so much! Thank you, and please, remember to be kind. Remember that love should never be made ugly.

Love hard, you all!

-Nicole